Clear

Expectations

A MARY O'REILLY PARANORMAL MYSTERY

(Book Twenty)

by

Terri Reid

CLEAR EXPECTATIONS

A MARY O'REILLY PARANORMAL MYSTERY
(BOOK 20)

by

Terri Reid

Copyright © 2017 by Terri Reid

The author would like to thank all those who have contributed to the creation of this book: Richard Reid, Sarah Powers and, the always amazing, Hillary Gadd. She would like to also thank Peggy Hannah, Mickey Claus, Terrie Snyder, Alex Boettcher and Nick Butzirus.

She would also like to thank all of the wonderful readers who have walked with her through Mary and Bradley's adventures and encouraged her along the way.

Prologue

The sounds from various New Year's Eve celebrations drifted from televisions in the individual patient rooms to the darkened hallway on the fourth floor of the hospital. Two nurses sat at the nurses station at the end of the hallway across from the elevator banks.

"It's quiet tonight," Mandy, a recently hired nurse, said. "Is that normal?"

The veteran nurse, Barbara, nodded. "Yes, holiday nights are usually pretty quiet," she explained. "And, thank goodness, the weather is good tonight, so we won't have as many car accidents down in ER."

Mandy looked around and sighed. "Is there anything you need me to do?" she asked. "I'm really kind of antsy."

Barbara chuckled and nodded. "Let me take a look," she said. She looked down at her inventory list, then turned to Mandy. "We're low on bedsheets," she said. "Would you mind grabbing ten more sheets from supplies?"

Mandy immediate stood up. "No problem," she said. "Where's supplies?"

"Take the elevators down one floor to three," Barb explained. "Once the doors open, you'll see a deserted nurses station on the right, just before the doors to an empty wing. That used to be pediatrics before we moved it to two. On the left, there's a locked door with supplies." Barbara opened a small drawer, fished out a set of keys and handed them to Mandy. "The key with the red dot is the one that opens the door."

"Thanks," Mandy said. "I'll be right back."

"Take your time," Barbara replied. "I don't expect a rush here."

Mandy took the elevator down. It only took a moment to go from four down to three. The elevator doors opened to a dimly lit floor. She walked out and glanced to her right. The empty nurses station was just down the hall before the double doors that she assumed led to the now empty rooms. There were a few boxes on the counter that surrounded the station, but other than those, the station was empty.

She turned to the left and saw the door with the word "Supplies" stenciled on it. Walking over to the doors, she pulled out the key and inserted it into the lock. A light switch was conveniently located right inside the door, and Mandy switched it on. Bright light flooded the interior of the supply room. Metal shelves lined up in narrow aisles throughout the small room. She easily located the sheets and also found a plastic tub she could use to carry them upstairs. She piled the sheets into the tub, carried them out of the room, then turned off the light and locked the door.

Hefting the tub back into her arms, she turned around and was surprised to see a little girl standing next to the empty nurses station. Mandy guessed the little girl was about eight years old. She had a hospital gown on and her hair was styled in two braids that hung on either side of her head. She must have wandered away from the pediatric ward on the second floor.

"Hey, sweetheart," she said. "I'm Mandy. Are you lost?"

The girl stared at her for a long moment but didn't answer.

"Come on. I can bring you back to your room," Mandy coaxed, not wanting to frighten the child.

The child didn't respond.

Mandy put the tub down and looked back up, but the child was gone. Shaking her head in surprise, Mandy slowly stepped forward, her heart thumping in her chest. The little girl must have dashed behind the counter. That had to be where she was. "Little girl," she called. "Where are you?"

She peeked behind the nurses station expecting to find the child hiding, but no one was there. All of the cabinets and desks that used to be behind the counter were gone, so just the shell of the counter stood around her. There was nowhere to hide. Nowhere to go.

A chill ran up Mandy's spine.

She backed away from the station, her mouth dry and her heart pounding. She grabbed the tub of sheets and dashed to the elevator, beating on the button in desperation, not daring to look over her shoulder at the wing behind her. Finally, the elevator doors opened, and she nearly tripped getting in she was so eager to leave the floor. She pressed the fourth-floor button and gasped with relief when the doors opened into the bright floor.

"What happened to you?" Barbara asked, looking at the expression on Mandy's face.

"Downstairs," Mandy gasped. "On the third floor. There was a little girl, and then she disappeared."

Barbara's mouth opened, and then she closed it. "I'm so sorry," she finally said. "I didn't even think to tell you about her."

"Her?" Mandy asked. "You mean what I saw was real?"

Barbara nodded. "Yes, people have seen the little girl ghost for years," she replied. "No one knows who she is or why she's still here."

"Well, I'm never going to get supplies in the middle of the night again," Mandy said, her voice still shaking. "That was the worst experience of my life."

Chapter One

A fire was crackling in the fireplace. The lights in the room were dimmed and the television was showing a picture of Times Square, the New Year's Ball still sparkling at the top of its flagpole. Bradley Alden looked down at his wife, Mary O'Reilly Alden, who was snuggled up against him on the couch and sound asleep.

He glanced at the timer in the corner of the television screen. Only five minutes remained until the countdown would start. He sighed. She had been so insistent about being awake for their first New Year's Eve celebration as husband and wife. But he really wanted to let her sleep.

She snored softly and burrowed a little further into his arm, and his heart melted a little more. He'd only known her for a little over a year and yet she'd changed his life completely. He leaned down and kissed her gently. She'd changed his life for the better. She had not only brought his daughter back into his life but also love, family and hope. She and her crazy, paranormal gift had rescued him.

And she wanted to celebrate their first New Year's Eve together. How could he refuse any request she had?

He leaned over. "Mary," he whispered softly. "Mary, it's almost time."

She mumbled in her sleep. "Hmmmmm?" she asked, her eyes still closed.

"It's almost time," he repeated.

Her eyes burst wide open, and she sat straight up. "Is the baby coming?" she asked, still half asleep.

"No, sweetheart," he said, chuckling softly while he pulled her back into his arms. "No, it's almost time for the ball to drop. You said you wanted me to wake you up."

Shaking her head, she looked up at Bradley. "Oh, wow," she was finally able to manage as she pushed her hair out of her eyes. "I was having this strange dream. You were pregnant and I was trying to get you to the hospital in time."

He kissed her forehead. "Did we make it in time?" he asked.

She smiled at him. "You woke me up just as we were getting into the car," she explained. "Now we'll never know."

"I hated to wake you up," he said.

She looked over to the television. "Oh! It's almost time!" she exclaimed. She smiled at him. "Our first New Years as a married couple."

He leaned forward and picked up a champagne glass of sparkling grape juice and handed it to her. Then he picked one up for himself. "I'm looking forward to many, many, many more," he said softly. "Have I told you how much I love you?"

"Not in the past thirty minutes," she said, a little breathless from the intensity of his gaze. "But, you know, I've been asleep."

"I love you, Mary O'Reilly Alden," he whispered and then kissed her.

"I love you, Bradley Alden," she replied, leaning up and kissing him back. He deepened the kiss, and Mary nearly dropped her glass.

Suddenly, the crowd on the screen started counting backwards. "Ten, nine, eight…"

They broke apart and Mary grinned. "We don't want to miss this," she teased.

"Five seconds," Bradley said pointedly.

"Four, three, two, one."

"Happy New Year," Mary said, tapping her glass against Bradley's glass and then sipping the frothy juice. "Well, Happy New York New Year."

"Happy New Year, sweetheart," he replied, sipping his own. Then he put his glass down on the coffee table and took Mary's from her and put it next to his. "Now, we have two choices."

"Two choices?" she asked, slightly breathless as she saw the desire in his eyes.

"Choice one. We can stay down here and try to stay awake for the Chicago New Year's celebration," he offered.

She slid her hands slowly up his chest, then leaned forward and nibbled on his chin. "And choice two?"

His eyes darkened, and he slid his hands slowly down her sides. "We can finish celebrating upstairs," he murmured, leaning over and placing soft, teasing kisses on her neck.

She felt the heat bubble through her system, felt her body respond to his touch. "You know," she said, her voice slightly trembling. "There have been studies that say too much television isn't good for a relationship."

He gently nibbled on her ear lobe, and she gasped. "Oh, my," she whispered. "I vote for choice two."

He nodded. "Good choice," he said. Standing, he bent down and lifted her up in his arms.

"Bradley, you're going to hurt yourself," she protested weakly.

"I think I can handle it," Bradley replied, carrying her across the room with ease. "Besides, I read that chicks really dig it when guys carry them."

She wrapped her arms around her neck and laughed. "Yes, chicks really do dig it," she said and then kissed his neck. "This chick especially."

He moved her towards the staircase, but her foot hit a tall, unlit candle on a hall table and sent it clattering to the floor. Bradley looked at the candle and then looked at Mary. "Oops," he said with a grin. "Good thing Clarissa is having a sleep-over with Maggie."

Mary grinned. "Good thing," she said. Then she paused and looked at him.

"What?" he asked.

"The fire is really romantic," she said. "And there's no one home but us..."

He smiled down at her, thought about it for a moment and then shook his head and continued towards the staircase. "But who knows who might decide to visit us in the middle of..." he wiggled his eyebrows suggestively.

"The night?" she giggled.

He stopped and looked down at his beautiful wife. Her eyes were alight with happiness and desire. Her lips were slightly swollen from his kisses. And her body was swollen with his child. He felt a wave of pure joy wash over him. He had to kiss her again, had to let her know just how much she meant to him.

"Mary," he whispered, his voice rough with emotion. "I love you." He tenderly kissed her, pouring his emotions into the mating of their mouths.

Mary felt heat pooling in her abdomen as he teased and tasted her. Humor fled and desire built. Finally, he ended the kiss slowly, unhurriedly sliding his lips over hers. When he lifted his head, he stared down into her eyes. "You are so beautiful," he finally said, his voice hoarse.

"We should go upstairs," she breathed. "Quickly."

He grinned down at her. "Yeah," he whispered. "I agree."

Chapter Two

Bradley woke up the next morning and was surprised to discover that he was alone in his bedroom. Dressed in the tartan flannel pajama bottoms Mary had given him for Christmas, he slipped from bed and hurried downstairs. He could smell the bacon when he was halfway down the staircase, and when he arrived in the kitchen, he stopped at the kitchen door in amazement. There were platters of bacon, pancakes, eggs and fruit on the counter. Mary's back was to him as she searched through the refrigerator.

"Are we expecting company?" he asked, coming up behind her and wrapping his arms around her waist.

She leaned back against him, looked up over her shoulder and smiled at him. "Good morning, sleepy head," she replied. "And no, we are not having company. It's just you and me." Then she looked down at her belly. "Oh, and Mikey."

He leaned forward and kissed her. "Good morning," he replied. "How did you sleep?"

"Like a rock," she said, enjoying the warmth of his arms around her. "I can't believe I woke up so early."

He shifted his hands and laid them on her belly. "And how's Mikey this morning?" he asked.

"Other than practicing river-dancing on my bladder, he's great," she said. She stayed in his arms for another moment, then sighed. "I suppose we should eat before everything gets cold."

He kissed her neck. "I don't mind cold food," he whispered.

She turned in his arms, shook her head and smiled up at him. "Stop that, Bradley Alden. We are going to eat warm food this morning," she said. She reluctantly slipped out of his arms, picked up two of the platters and brought them to the table.

Bradley picked up the other two and followed her. Then he pulled out a chair for her. "You sit down," he insisted. "I'll get the rest of the things from the counter."

She sat down and placed a couple of strips of bacon on her plate. "I heard from Rosie this morning," she said, biting the end off one of the pieces. "She said that Stanley is as cranky as ever."

Bringing the milk, butter and syrup over, Bradley placed them on the table. "So, he's feeling better?" he asked, sitting down next to her.

She chuckled. "Yes, he must be," she replied. "He's still got a way to go, but his burns seem to be healing and they don't think he's going to need heart surgery."

"That's great news," he said, filling his plate. "Do they know when he's going to be released?"

"Not for another couple of weeks," she said. "They want the burns to heal before he can come home."

"So, you both might be in the hospital at the same time," he replied as he poured syrup on his pancakes.

"No," Mary said. "Mikey isn't due until the twentieth. Stanley will be out before that."

"But what if Mikey comes early?"

Mary sighed. "The doctor said not to even think about the baby coming early," she reminded him. "Early babies are rare for first-time moms."

Bradley smiled at her. "Okay, Stanley out and you in," he said. "How's Rosie doing?"

"Honestly, I think Stanley is driving her nuts," she chuckled. "He's bored, so he's cranky. So, I thought I'd bring over some board games and give Rosie a break."

"Bring the Texas Hold 'Em poker set," Bradley suggested. "The way you play poker, you could win enough money to pay for a new addition to the house."

"You want me to fleece Stanley while he's in the hospital?" she asked with a smile. "Whatever will Rosie say?"

Bradley shrugged. "Well, you could get a couple of those rich doctors pulled into the game," he said with a grin. "It wouldn't take you long to win a couple grand."

She chuckled. "You have such confidence in my poker playing abilities," she said.

"Well, you beat the pants off me," he replied. "Literally."

She smiled and lightly bit her lower lip. "Well, there was quite a bit of incentive there," she said, winking at him. "You do have sexy legs."

Bradley grinned and shrugged casually. "Well, you know, I do work out…"

"And you're a really crappy poker player," she added with a grin. "Really crappy."

The grin slipped from Bradley's face. "Well, thanks for sparing my feelings," he replied, taking a bite of pancakes.

Her smile widened. "I did say you have sexy legs," she teased then took a bite of pancakes too. For a moment, there was no conversation.

"So, what are you going to do today?" she finally asked.

"I'm going to finish getting the guest room set up," he said. "I want everything ready for your mom."

"You are my hero," she said. "Mom's pretty excited about being here when Mikey's born." She hesitated and glanced over at him. "Tell me the truth. Do you mind?"

Bradley reached over and placed his hand on hers. "I love you, and I want you to have everything and everyone you need," he said. "And, I have to admit, having your mom in the room will make me feel a lot less nervous about this whole thing."

"Yeah," Mary agreed. "Me too."

Chapter Three

Mary pulled her car into the parking lot at the hospital and parked near the side entrance. In the back seat of her SUV she had a large shopping bag filled with games she thought Stanley would enjoy. Putting the car into park, she opened the door and pushed herself out, making sure she was completely balanced before she allowed her eight-month pregnant body to move forward. She tested the ground to make sure it wasn't icy, and when she determined it was only wet, she stepped forward.

Never before in her life had she been this cautious. She had always been more of the "act first, ask questions later" kind of person. But as this new little life moved and kicked within her, she felt an overwhelming feeling of protection and prudence. She didn't want to be the cause of anything harming her child.

She lifted the bag from the back of the seat, locked the car and walked toward the side entrance. The large, glass, revolving door moved slowly forward, and Mary longed to push it, just a little, to speed things up. But she bit back her impatience and slowed her pace to match the door's movement. Finally, she stepped out of the door and walked to the receptionist's desk.

"Excuse me," she said with a smile. "I'm here…"

The young receptionist looked up at Mary and her eyes widened in alarm. "Oh, dear," she exclaimed. "Just have a seat and we'll be right with you."

She pointed to a leather chair next to the desk. Mary shrugged and sat down, watching the receptionist pick up the phone and repeat a code.

"Is everything all right?" Mary asked.

The receptionist smiled and nodded, looking a little harried. "Oh, yes, just fine," she replied, her voice squeaking in excitement. "Someone will be here for you in just a moment."

"Perhaps there's been a mistake," Mary offered. "I'm here…"

The receptionist shook her head and laughed nervously. "Oh, no, I can see why you're here," she said. The phone rang. She picked it up and then turned back to Mary. "They want to know how close they're coming."

Mary shook her head. "I'm sorry. How close who are coming?" she asked.

"Your contractions," the receptionist replied, rolling her eyes. "How close are your contractions coming?"

Mary sighed. "I'm not having contractions," Mary said. "I'm here to see a friend."

The receptionist stared at her for a long moment, then turned away from her and spoke through the phone. "Cancel the wheelchair," she said, her voice heavy with disgust. "She just told me that she's not in labor. Which would have been nice to know several minutes ago."

Mary stood up and leaned over towards the receptionist, bumping her belly against the edge of the desk. "If you had given me a chance, I would have told you sooner," Mary replied pointedly, a smile still plastered on her face.

The young receptionist looked surprised, as if she didn't think Mary could hear her. "I'm sorry," she replied. "This is a private conversation."

Mary shook her head, turned and walked away from the desk. With her teeth clenched, she marched away towards the elevators. She'd find her own way up to Stanley's new room, and nobody better give her a hard time. She stopped in front of the elevators and poked the button, venting a little on the innocent plastic knob.

"I'm sorry," she muttered. "This is a private conversation."

"Excuse me?" an elderly man behind her asked.

Embarrassed, Mary shook her head. "Oh, I'm sorry," she said. "Just muttering to myself."

The door opened, and they both entered the elevator. He pressed the button for the fourth floor immediately, but Mary pondered her decision for a moment.

"Um, psychiatric offices are on two," he suggested helpfully as he moved as far away from her as possible.

The laughter escaped before she could stop it. Breathless, leaning against the elevator wall, she hit the button for the second floor and continued to laugh. The door opened, and she glanced behind her before she exited the elevator. The poor man had a horrified look on his face.

"Have a nice day," Mary gasped before stepping out onto the floor. She continued to laugh as the door closed behind her, then finally, catching her breath, turned around to see a nurse at the station behind her.

"May I help you?" the nurse asked kindly.

"I really need to find a bathroom," Mary confessed. "And then, is there any way you can help me locate a friend's room?"

The nurse smiled. "Of course," she said. "Here, there's a bathroom right down the hall. Why don't you tell me your friend's name and I'll look it up while you're in there."

"Stanley," Mary said as she hurried down the hall. "Stanley Wagner."

Chapter Four

"Dagnabbit," Stanley called out, throwing his cards on the hospital table in front of him. "This just ain't normal." He narrowed his eyes and stared at Mary. "You got those cards marked?"

She smiled and shrugged. "Wouldn't you like to know," she taunted. "Okay, well, now you owe me your mansion in Tuscany."

"Well, Rosie ain't gonna be all too happy about that," he grumbled, biting back a smile. "You already got the condo in Aspen and the vineyard in France."

"You got to know when to hold 'em, know when to fold 'em," Mary started singing as she made dance movements with her arms.

"Did you lose again, Stanley?" Mandy, his nurse, asked, pushing a cart in front of her as she entered the room.

"Dang-blasted card shark just won my mansion in Tuscany," he complained, and then he turned to Mary and smiled wickedly. "Just so you know, it's haunted. Some whiny I-talian ghost who walks around with his head in his arms."

Mary shrugged. "I'm not afraid of any ghost," she said with a smile. "Even a headless Italian."

Mandy shivered. "Well, if you had seen what I saw, you'd be afraid," she said.

Mary turned to look at her. "You saw a ghost?" she asked.

"Yes, last night," Mandy replied. "On the third floor in the old pediatric wing."

"What happened?" Mary asked.

"Oh, no," Stanley interrupted. "You are s'posed to be concentrating on relaxing and getting ready for that there baby. You ain't got time to do any more ghostbusting."

"Are you one of those paranormal investigators?" Mandy asked, her voice tinged with excitement.

"Well, yes and no," Mary replied. "I have been known to be sensitive to ghosts."

Stanley snorted.

"Tell me what happened," Mary urged.

"Well, I went downstairs to get some sheets from the supply closet," she explained. "When I came out and turned around, there she was, standing next to the nurses station."

"What did she look like?" Mary asked.

"She was a little girl," Mandy said. "She looked to be about eight years old. She had the saddest face…"

Stanley threw his hands up in the air. "Oh, now she's hooked," he grumbled.

Mary turned back to Stanley. "Shhhh," she scolded.

"At first, I thought she was a patient," Mandy continued. "And, you know, she'd gotten lost. So, I approached her and asked her if I could help her. She didn't say a word. I looked away for a moment, and then she was just gone."

"I betcha you hightailed it back up the elevator lickety-split after that," Stanley said with a twinkle in his eye.

She smiled and nodded. "I hit that elevator button so many times, I'm surprised it still works," she replied with a laugh. "When I got back I told Barbara. She was the senior floor nurse last night, and she said, 'Oh, yeah, a lot of people have seen her.'"

"It woulda been nice for her to warn you," Stanley said.

Mandy nodded. "That's what I was thinking too," she agreed. She moved over and placed the blood pressure cuff around Stanley's arm. "But I don't know if I would have believed her."

"So, she's been around for a long time?" Mary asked.

Mandy nodded. "Yeah, sounds like twenty years or so," she said. "All the old-timers here at the hospital either have heard about her or have seen her themselves. I think that's one of the reasons they decided to gut the pediatric area and move it to another floor. Too many patients were making friends with the ghost."

"Do you know who she is?" Mary asked.

Mandy shook her head. "No, I guess they've tried to look up records," she said as she slipped her stethoscope in place. "But no such luck."

Mandy efficiently checked all of Stanley's vitals, gave him his afternoon medications, checked his IV and then went back to the cart. "Well, good luck with your card game," she said with a smile. She winked at Mary. "I'd try for the cabin in Sun Valley next."

"Hey, you're supposed to be helping me," Stanley complained.

Mary laughed. "Thanks for the tip, Mandy," she said. "And good luck with the ghost."

Mandy shook her head. "Oh, no, I've decided that someone else can get supplies," she said. "One sighting was enough for me."

Once Mandy pulled the door closed behind her, Stanley leaned forward in his bed. "Listen here, missy," he said. "Don't go looking for trouble. She didn't come to you, so she ain't looking to leave."

"But, Stanley, she's only a little girl," Mary argued. "A lost and sad little girl."

"And that crazy psychopath what done this to me was only a little boy," Stanley replied firmly. "'Lessen Mike gives the okay, you stay away from that third floor, you hear?"

She nodded. "Yes, Stanley," she said. "I hear."

Chapter Five

A half hour later, Rosie came into Stanley's room wreathed in smiles. "The nurses here are the sweetest people in the world," she said. "Don't you think so?"

"Not when they're poking and prodding me in places ain't no one got a right to touch," he grumbled.

"Obviously they think they do," Mary said, biting back a smile. "And I agree with Rosie. They are the sweetest people in the world. Mandy is adorable."

Stanley shrugged. "Well, okay, you got a point there," he grudgingly admitted. "She's the only one what shows a little respect to an ill patient."

Rosie looked alarmed. "What?" she squeaked, looking quickly around the room. "Who hasn't been showing you respect?"

Mary stood up from her chair next to the bed and chuckled. "I think our ill patient is a sore loser,"

Mary teased. Then she looked Stanley in the eye. "Next time we play for your car."

Stanley folded his arms over his chest in indignation, but his eyes were twinkling with mirth. "Ain't gonna be a next time, you card shark," he growled. "Fool me once, shame on you."

Mary shook her head, then bent over and kissed Stanley on the cheek. "It's not fooling," she said. "It's skill."

"Just 'cause you can lie like a dog and look all innocent," Stanley countered. "It's not a skill."

Mary laughed. "Are you kidding?" she replied. "It's one of the best skills you can have."

She hurried over and gave Rosie a hug. "Good luck," she whispered into Rosie's ear. "I think I might have tired him out for you."

"You are an angel," she whispered back. "I haven't seen him so lively in days."

Mary stepped away from Rosie and turned back to Stanley. "Get your dictionary out and start studying," she said. "Tomorrow we play Scrabble, and I might give you a chance to win back some of your real estate."

"But, Scrabble isn't a betting game," Rosie said.

Grinning, Mary wiggled her eyebrows. "Any game worth playing is a game worth betting on," she replied. "Right, Stanley?"

"That's right, girlie," he said. "And just you wait. I got words in this here mind you ain't never even heard of."

"As long as you didn't make them up in that there mind," Mary replied.

Stanley laughed out loud before he could help himself. Then he shook his head. "Get out of here so an old man can get some sleep," he said, trying to hold back more laughter.

"Old man my foot," Mary said. "I'll go. But I know you're just hurrying me out of here so you can figure out a way to beat me tomorrow." She winked at Rosie. "See you later."

She closed the door behind her but not before she heard Stanley's voice. "Rosie, help me download the dictionary app to my phone."

Chuckling, she hurried down the hall towards the elevator. She glanced at her own phone and saw that she had an hour before Clarissa would be getting home from the Brennans' house. She thought about the things she needed to do before going home— a quick stop at the grocery store and then a stop to fill up her vehicle with gas. She stepped onto the elevator and stared at the buttons for a long moment.

With a quick breath, she pressed the button for the third floor.

"Probably nothing will happen," she said to herself as the door closed and the elevator made its way down one story. She started to step out when Stanley's words came back to haunt her. "That crazy psychopath what done this to me was only a little boy."

"That was a unique experience," she argued with herself as she placed her hand on the door to keep it from closing. "All the other children ghosts were—"

"Can I help you?"

Mary jumped and squealed in fright. Turning, she saw a nurse standing in the lobby with the supply room door wide open.

"I'm so sorry," Mary began. But before she could say another word, the nurse was at her side.

"Don't worry. You just took the wrong elevator," the nurse said calmly. "I'll get you to maternity right away. How far apart are the contractions?"

Chapter Six

Mike laughed loudly as he floated across the living room floor toward Mary.

"It wasn't that funny," Mary grumbled. "I'm getting pretty tired of…"

"Being mistaken for a pregnant woman?" Mike inserted with glee. "Yeah, I can totally see that. What are people thinking anyway?"

She glared at him. "You're not helping," she said. "I already feel as big as a barn…"

"Surely not a barn," Mike said, eyeing her slowly up and down. "I'd say a small residential house. A cottage, even."

"Can angels die twice?" Mary threatened.

He chuckled. "Come on, Mary," he urged. "Lighten up. You only have a few more weeks…"

He froze, but it was too late. Mary's eyes widened with interest.

"Do you know something?" she asked. "Do you have some inside information? Is Mikey coming early?"

Mike shook his head. "No, nothing," he said. "Babies come when they're supposed to."

She stepped up closer and looked into his eyes. "You do know!" she exclaimed. "Why won't you tell me so I can stop worrying?"

He shook his head. "Sorry, classified information," he said. "A need to know situation."

Mary looked down at her bulging belly and then looked up at him, incredulous. "And you don't think I have a need to know?"

He stepped closer, his smile gone, replaced with tender concern. "I'm sorry, Mar," he began. "I'm not…"

She smiled at him and sighed. "Yeah, I get it," she replied. "But, you know, if you could just see if they'll make an exception…"

He nodded. "Yeah, I'll ask," he said. "I'll even get slightly annoying about it."

Mary opened her eyes wide again. "What? You get annoying? That couldn't happen."

He grinned. "Keep it up and I'll talk to them about teaching you patience," he said, and then he slowly started to fade away.

"What's so bad about learning patience?" she asked to his nearly invisible form.

"The elephant used to have the same gestational period as the human being," he said. "Until she asked to learn patience."

"What?" Mary yelled into the now empty room. "Mike that's not fair! Mike get back here."

"Gotta go," Mike's disembodied voice floated around the room. "Oh, and by the way, you can check out the third floor of the hospital. They've been waiting a long time."

"They?" Mary whispered. "They?"

She glanced at the clock. Clarissa would be home in a few minutes.

The knock on the front door surprised her. She hurried over and pulled it open to see her mother, Margaret O'Reilly, standing on the front porch.

"Mom!" she exclaimed, throwing her arms around her.

Margaret wrapped her arms around her daughter and just held her. "Happy New Year, sweetheart. I know I wasn't supposed to arrive yet," she said. "But I just couldn't stand waiting."

Mary laughed joyfully, her eyes filled with tears. "This is perfect!" she cried. "Absolutely perfect."

She stepped back, smiling, and took a deep breath. "And Bradley fixed the room for you this morning, so it's ready," she said.

"Well, isn't he a brilliant son-in-law?" Margaret laughed.

"He's as nervous as me about the baby coming," Mary admitted. "So we will all sleep a lot better knowing that you're here."

"Well, I'm glad to hear it," Margaret admitted. "I was a little worried you'd turn me away and send me back to Chicago."

"Not a chance," Mary said, putting her arm around her mother's shoulders and guiding her inside. "Not a chance."

Chapter Seven

"Grandma, I'm so glad you're finally here," Clarissa exclaimed as they sat around the table that evening.

Margaret smiled at her new granddaughter. "I'm so glad I'm finally here too," she replied with a soft chuckle. "I haven't seen you since Christmas, and it seems like forever."

Bradley bit back a chuckle and nodded. "Forever," he repeated.

Clarissa nodded. "Christmas was a long, long, long time ago," she agreed. "Grandma, you need to move next door."

"That would be a wonderful thing," Margaret agreed with twinkle in her eye. "But I would really miss Grandpa."

Clarissa shook her head. "Oh, no, Grandpa would move here too," she insisted. "He would have to!"

"That would be wonderful," Mary agreed. "You and Dad would love Freeport."

"Well, I'll be sure to discuss it with him," Margaret promised. "But I don't think he's ever going to retire." She turned her attention to Clarissa. "So, when do you go back to school?"

"On Tuesday," the little girl replied with a sigh. "We only get one day to celebrate New Year's."

"But you've already had two weeks off school," Bradley reminded her. "And if you stay out any longer, you're going to forget everything you learned so far."

Sighing dramatically, Clarissa looked at her father. "If I didn't forget everything during the summer, I won't forget everything during Christmas break," she explained.

"But it's winter," Bradley argued. "So, it's cold and your brain doesn't work as well. It freezes things out."

"Really?" Clarissa asked Mary.

Margaret laughed. "Ah, I see she knows who does the teasing in this household."

Mary smiled at her daughter. "No, that's not quite true," she replied. "But you love school, don't you? You love your teacher and your friends."

"I guess," Clarissa said. "But with Grandma here, it would be more fun to be home."

"Well, tomorrow I'll be here, and you'll have the day off," Margaret offered. "Shall we make a day of it?"

"Really?" Clarissa asked, her eyes filled with excitement.

"Really," Margaret replied, then stopped and looked over at Mary and Bradley. "That is if it's fine with your parents."

"I think that's a great idea," Bradley said. "Thank you."

"I love the idea too," Mary said. "Just the two of you."

"Can we have just the three of us?" Clarissa asked. "Maggie is coming over tomorrow, remember?"

"Oh, that's right," Mary replied. She had totally forgotten about her promise to Katie that she would have Maggie over. "I'm sorry, honey. Let's schedule a you and Grandma day another time."

Margaret saw the disappointment in Clarissa's eyes and turned to Mary. "Why?" she asked. "Is there something you had planned to do with the girls, or could I just add Maggie to our day?"

"I really didn't have anything planned yet," Mary replied. "Are you sure you don't mind?"

"Mind?" Margaret laughed. "I think it would be delightful to have both girls with me. How about you, Clarissa?"

"It would be so much fun," Clarissa said. "And I know Maggie would love it too."

"Well then," Margaret said. "It's a date. We'll have to find an adventure."

Clarissa wiggled excitedly in her chair. "I love adventure!" she exclaimed. "Especially when you're part of it."

Margaret laughed. "And I love an adventure that you're a part of, so we're even."

Chapter Eight

"I can't believe she asked to go to bed. It's not even eight o'clock," Mary said as she, Bradley and Margaret were sitting together in the living room, the fireplace snapping as a warm fire blazed. Mary and Margaret shared the couch, and Bradley sat across from them in the recliner.

"She spent the night at Maggie's last night?" Margaret asked. "For New Year's Eve?"

"Yes," Mary replied. "Why?"

Margaret smiled. "Well, if she is anything like you, she didn't get any sleep at all last night," she teased kindly. "They probably spent the whole night talking about very important things."

Bradley laughed. "That sounds just like them," he said. "They are inseparable. They've already decided to work together when they grow up."

"Oh, really?" Margaret asked. "And what do they want to do?"

"Well, Clarissa wants to go into law enforcement," Mary said.

Margaret sighed. "Well, really, how could she not with this family," she said. "And Maggie?"

"Maggie has Mary's gift," Bradley explained. "She's been able to see ghosts and, even at her young age, help them. So…"

"They want to be like the two of you," Margaret exclaimed as the truth dawned on her. "They are just emulating you." She paused and smiled at them. "Well, you must be proud of them."

"Frightened to death is more like it," Mary said. "Why can't they both want to be supermodels or athletes like most girls their age?"

Laughing softly, Margaret shook her head. "Because most girls their age don't live with people who are heroes in their own right," she said with a casual shrug. "You've both set a fine example."

Mary met her mother's eyes. "You always made it seem so effortless," Mary finally said.

"What?" Margaret asked.

"Being an example," Mary replied. "You always seemed to know what to do, how to do it and how to handle things."

Margaret laughed. "Well, that's the greatest secret of parenting," she said, lowering her voice conspiringly. "Never, ever, let them see you sweat."

Bradley laughed. "Well, okay, I've already lost then," he said. "I'm constantly worried that I'm not doing the right thing. Being a parent is the most terrifying thing I've ever done."

"Aye, it is," Margaret agreed. "And the most satisfying." Her eyes moistened slightly. "Seeing your children grow up to be fine adults, raising their own children with love. That's a blessing to be sure."

Mary reached over and squeezed her mother's hand. "Thank you, Ma," she whispered. "I just always think, 'What would Ma do?'"

Margaret laughed. "And that will get you into all kinds of trouble."

"Speaking of trouble," Mary said with a smile. "I played poker with Stanley most of the afternoon. I won his cabin in Sun Valley, his mansion in Tuscany, his condo in Aspen and his vineyard in France."

"So, I can quit my job tomorrow and we can live off the sale of his property?" Bradley teased.

"I don't think so," Mary replied with a chuckle. "But it was fun to get him all worked up about losing to me."

"Kept his mind off being in the hospital?" Margaret asked.

Mary nodded. "Yes, and it gave Rosie a couple of hours of free time," she said. "Even though she's devoted to Stanley, I'm sure she was going a little stir crazy."

"How's Stanley doing?" Bradley asked.

"His vitals are all good, his appetite is back and he's complaining about the nursing staff," Mary reported.

"How are the nurses?" Margaret asked.

"Amazing. We had a new one, Mandy, who was just so sweet," Mary answered. "She actually just had a paranormal experience last night and told us about it."

"Someone told you about a ghost sighting?" Bradley exclaimed. "How unusual."

"Well, this one happened to her in the hospital, on the third floor," Mary said. "She was working last night and went down to get supplies. When she looked up, she saw a little girl standing next to the empty nurses station. She initially thought the child was a misplaced patient, but when the little girl disappeared before her eyes…"

"Did you go down to the third floor on your way home?" Margaret asked.

Mary smiled. "I did," she said. "Just to peek. But there was a nurse down there in the supply area, so I just came home."

Margaret studied her daughter for a long moment and then she smiled. "I think you and Bradley ought to go and visit Stanley for a few minutes tonight," she suggested. "I'm here for Clarissa. And, if you both happen to accidentally press the button for the third floor instead of the fourth, who knows who you might find."

"Really?" Mary asked. "You wouldn't mind?"

Margaret's smile widened. "I have a feeling that you won't sleep very well until you figure out why that little girl is still there."

Mary leaned over and kissed her mother. "Thanks, Ma. You're wonderful."

"And a mind reader," Bradley added. "Thank you, Margaret."

"You're both welcome," she replied. "Now go and solve a mystery."

Chapter Nine

Bradley stepped off the elevator before Mary
and looked down the dimly lit corridor on the third
floor. "I think I've seen this movie before," he
whispered over his shoulder. "And it doesn't end
well."

Mary giggled. "Stop it," she said. "I already
have to go to the bathroom and I don't want to laugh.
It makes it worse."

He turned around. "You have to go to the
bathroom?" he asked, feigning surprise.

"Shut up," she replied.

Bradley chuckled. "Well, I'm sure there's a
bathroom around here," he said, stepping forward
into the lobby area.

Mary followed him, peering around. Only the
emergency lights were lit, and the rest of the hall was
filled with gloomy shadows. "It's pretty spooky
down here," she said.

Bradley stopped and looked at her. "Since
when are you worried about spooky?" he asked.

She sighed. "It's weird," she replied. "I don't know if it's because Mikey is coming so soon, or my ability to run and protect myself has been greatly reduced, or my emotions are on overdrive, but I'm easily spooked these days."

Nodding, Bradley put his arm around her shoulders. "That makes sense," he said. "So, let's take this slow and easy. Why don't we find a bathroom first, and since this floor is deserted, I'll go in with you and wait outside the stall."

"Really?" she asked.

He grinned down at her. "Of course," he said. "I always wanted to see what was inside a girl's bathroom anyway."

She laughed. "You are so weird," she teased.

"And yet, you married me," he replied.

They walked down the hallway, and when it got too dim, Mary pulled a flashlight out of her purse to brighten the area.

"What else do you have in there?" Bradley asked, motioning to her purse.

Mary grinned. "Just wait until I start carrying a diaper bag," she replied. "Then I'll be fully armed."

A sign on the wall indicated a women's bathroom, and Bradley opened the door to look inside. The fixtures were all in place. "Looks good," he said. "Let me check and make sure the water's on."

He walked over and turned on a faucet and water poured out.

"Oh!" Mary squealed. "The sound of running water didn't help. Gotta go."

She slipped quickly into a stall and Bradley reached over and turned off the water. "Sorry about that," he called, biting back his laughter.

"Oh, yeah, you think you're so funny," Mary called from within the stall.

Still chucking softly, Bradley looked around the room. There were probably eight stalls along one side of the room and four large sinks directly across from them. A mirror ran the length of the room over the sinks. In the dim light, he could barely make out his reflection in the mirror and chuckled when light burst from inside the stall Mary was in.

"Got a little dark in there?" he called.

"Funny!" she replied. "I'm looking for toilet paper, but I can't find any in here."

"I'll check the other stalls," he called back.

He went into the first stall and only found cardboard rolls. The second stall was the same. Mary was in the third stall, so he moved on to the fourth. As he approached the door, he happened to glance at the mirror, and then he froze, staring at his reflection. He could see himself, but next to his image was the reflection of a little girl in a hospital gown. He watched in the mirror as she lifted her hand and touched his hand. A shock of pure cold traveled up his arm, and then she disappeared.

"Bradley," Mary called out. "Are you okay?"

It took him a moment to answer. "Yeah," he breathed, his heart pounding in his chest. "Yeah, I'm good. But, um, I just met the little girl the nurse was talking about."

"You did?" Mary exclaimed.

"Yeah, she appeared next to me and then touched my hand," he replied.

"Okay, you need to hurry and get me some toilet paper because I don't want her to appear in the stall with me."

Bradley laughed, feeling some of the tension slip away, and checked the next stall. "We have a winner," he said, pulling the roll from the next stall and handing it to Mary.

"Thank goodness," Mary said. "Because there was no way I was going to let you leave this bathroom to go search somewhere else."

She came out a few minutes later and hurried to the sink. He stood behind her, watching for any signs of the child. "What I don't understand," Bradley said as Mary washed her hands and pulled a bottle of hand sanitizer from her purse, "is how with all that other stuff in your purse, you don't have tissues."

"Oh, I …" she stopped and looked up at him, biting softly on her lower lip. "I forgot."

He shook his head and then bent down and kissed her. "Actually, considering the circumstances, I would have forgotten too," he said. "So, shall we continue the search?"

Mary nodded. "Yes," she said. "Especially now that she's contacted you."

Chapter Ten

Slipping past the deserted nurses station, Mary and Bradley pushed open the large, swinging doors that led to the old pediatric unit. The doors swished closed behind them, causing a chill to run down Mary's spine.

"Are you okay?" Bradley asked.

She nodded silently, her eyes slowly scanning the long hallway before her. "I can feel someone in here with us," she whispered.

Instantly remembering their encounter in the asylum, Bradley put his arm around Mary and turned her to him. "Do you feel anything like you felt in the asylum?" he asked urgently.

She paused for a moment, letting the energy from the unit wash over her, and then shook her head. "No. No, it's not evil or aggressive," she replied softly. "There's sadness and...fear. Yes, there's definitively a feeling of fear here."

"Fear of you?" Bradley asked. "Or just fear of the hospital?"

She met his eyes. "Just fear," she said. "I can't pin it down. But let's keep going."

They slowly walked down the corridor, pausing at each doorway and looking into the empty rooms.

"Do you see anything?" Bradley asked as they stood in one of the empty rooms. The closet doors were open, the shelves dusty but empty. The walls had blocks of lighter color where shelving must have been attached in the past. The floor was linoleum with a thin coating of plaster dust from some of the remodeling that had taken place. The windows had beige shades pulled down over them.

Mary slowly turned in a circle, studying each corner of the room, and then shook her head. "I'm catching quick glimpses out of the corner of my eye," she said. "But no one is appearing to me. No one is asking me for help."

"Isn't that strange?" he asked. "Aren't they supposed to be drawn to you?"

"Well, fear is a pretty primal emotion," Mary said. "And when you're filled with fear, all other emotions— love, trust, hope— can't get through. Fear paralyzes you."

"So, how do you move past that?" he asked.

She smiled and shrugged. "Faith," she replied. "Faith is like that little speck of light in a darkened room. When you stand there with the light, your eyes adjust and the light seems to get brighter. The darkness fades a little bit more. You are able to see things you hadn't seen before. You don't have to do much, just have a little bit of faith, and the fear will dissipate a little at a time."

"Okay, Mary, so what do we actually do? Bradley asked.

Mary shrugged. "Now we have to figure out what will inspire faith in this little girl."

They walked out of the room and continued to the end of the hall. "Is this strange?" Mary asked, noticing another hallway behind a wooden door with a glass window. "I've never seen a separate hallway like this before in other parts of the hospital."

Bradley reached down and grabbed hold of the doorknob, but the door was locked. He turned to

Mary. "A locked door in a pediatric ward?" he said. "That seems a little out of the ordinary. And why is it still locked?"

"Well, it could have been an isolation ward," she suggested. "And the lock is to keep people safe."

He nodded. "Yeah, it could have been," he said.

He stared at the door for a long moment. "I'm going to try something," he said. "Maybe since she reached out, I can get her to appear."

"Okay," Mary replied. "Great idea."

"Hello," he called out. "I'm here to help you. I'm not here to hurt you. I just want to understand why you're in the hospital."

They waited in silence for a few minutes. Mary reached over and took Bradley's hand in her own. Finally, he shook his head and sighed. "It didn't work," he said sadly. "I guess we should go home."

He started to turn away when he heard a shuffling sound. Mary shined her flashlight down and watched in surprise as a manila folder slid from underneath the locked door to just in front of their feet. Bradley bent down and picked it up. Mary turned the flashlight to the folder.

"It's a medical chart," he said, scanning the yellowed pages. Then he looked up and met Mary's eyes. "But it's for a little boy."

"What?" she asked. "But I thought—"

Suddenly a burst of childish laughter came from the other side of the door. They could hear several children laughing, their voices echoing in the dark, empty halls. Mary rubbed her arms as a chill ran up her spine.

"I think this is a little more complicated than we thought," Bradley said.

Mary nodded. "Yes, a little more crowded."

Chapter Eleven

Clarissa quietly opened her bedroom door and padded to the bathroom. She was a little surprised to discover that the hallway light was still on, and she wondered how late it really was. Once she had finished in the bathroom, she wandered over to the staircase. She could hear voices coming from downstairs. It must not be as late as she thought.

She started down the stairs when she heard her grandmother's voice.

"Oh, my, how frightening. More than one ghost on the third floor."

Knowing the conversation would probably stop if she continued downstairs, she stepped back up and crouched down next to the railing.

"There were at least a handful of children's voices coming from the other side of that door," she heard her mother say. "But none of them would show themselves to us."

"Why not?" her grandmother asked.

"We don't know," her father said. "My guess is that adults frighten them."

"I agree," her mother added. "If we could only get through to them and find out why they're still there."

Clarissa sat up straight. She could help. The ghost children wouldn't be afraid of her. She nearly ran down the stairs until she heard her father speaking.

"Let's not talk about this in front of Clarissa. It might be upsetting for her to hear about ghost children."

She slowly backed away from the staircase and then turned and ran back into her bedroom. She climbed into her bed and scrambled over to the other side. Reaching over to the nightstand on that side, she opened the top drawer and pulled out a small walkie-talkie. Rolling back to her pillows, she switched it on and pressed the button on the side.

"Maggie. Maggie. Are you there?" she called into the walkie-talkie.

"Do you know how late it is?" Maggie's sleepy voice replied.

"No, I don't" Clarissa replied honestly. "I just had to call you."

"Why?" Maggie asked.

"We have an adventure," she said.

"What kind of adventure?" Maggie asked skeptically.

"A ghost adventure," Clarissa replied. "I know a way we can help."

"This better be good," Maggie said.

"It will be," Clarissa replied. "I promise."

Chapter Twelve

"Good morning," Clarissa called down from upstairs just before she skipped happily down the steps.

"Good morning, sweetheart," Margaret said, meeting her at the foot of the stairs and hugging her. "Are you ready for our adventure?"

Clarissa nodded eagerly. "Yes, I'm so excited and so is Maggie," she replied.

"When did you talk to Maggie?" Mary asked.

Clarissa's face dropped. "Oh. I mean, I'm sure she will be happy," Clarissa replied.

Margaret and Mary exchanged doubtful glances at Clarissa's response. "Well, I'm sure she will be too," Margaret said. "I was thinking we could go to the craft store and then go out for lunch—"

"Grandma," Clarissa interrupted. "I was wondering if maybe we could go to the hospital and visit Grandpa Stanley instead."

Margaret stepped back and stared at Clarissa for a moment. "Really?" she asked, flabbergasted. "You would rather go and visit Grandpa Stanley than go to lunch?"

"Is that okay?" Clarissa asked, looking uncomfortable.

Margaret wrapped her arms around her granddaughter and hugged her tightly. "I think it's just wonderful," she whispered, her voice thick with emotion. "And so sweet. I can't imagine a more selfless decision."

"So it's okay?" Clarissa asked again.

Margaret laughed and hugged her once more. "Yes, it's just fine," she said. She turned to Mary. "Can Stanley have young visitors?"

Mary nodded. "Yes, as long as they are with you, they can visit," she said, walking over to them. "And I can't tell you how proud I am of you."

Clarissa looked down at her feet. "Thanks, Mom," she said softly.

"What's all this about?" Bradley asked, buttoning his uniform shirt as he walked down the stairs.

"Mom was going to take Clarissa and Maggie to the craft store and then out to lunch today," Mary began, "but Clarissa asked if they could go to the hospital and visit Stanley instead."

Bradley looked at his daughter and smiled proudly. "Wow, I am so impressed," he said. "Are you sure you want to give up your special day to visit Stanley?"

"Bradley!" Mary exclaimed. "Don't talk her out of it."

"Sorry," Bradley said. "I didn't mean it to sound that way. I'm just really surprised…in a good way."

Clarissa shrugged. "It's no big deal," she insisted.

"No, sweetheart," Bradley said, putting his hand on her shoulder. "It's a really big deal. And it shows me how much you're growing up."

The doorbell ringing interrupted their conversation, and Clarissa quickly excused herself from the adults. "It's Maggie," she said. "I'll get it."

She ran to the door and opened it.

"What did they say?" Maggie whispered.

"Wait a minute," Clarissa replied softly. Then she turned back towards the room of adults. "Is it okay if Maggie and I go upstairs to my room for a little bit? We want to make some get well cards for Stanley."

"Oh sure, sweetheart," Mary said. "That would be so nice."

Clarissa led Maggie up to her room and closed the door behind them.

"What's up?" Maggie asked.

"They said we could visit the hospital," Clarissa replied softly. "But, everyone's making a big deal about it, so I'm kind of feeling bad."

"Don't feel bad," Maggie reassured her quietly. "We are doing a good thing, in the long run."

Clarissa sighed. "Yeah, I suppose so," she said. "But I still feel kind of bad."

69

"Once we figure out what those ghost kids want, we'll be heroes again," Maggie said. "Besides, it was all your idea."

"Yeah, I guess," Clarissa agreed. "And if we want to do this when we're grown up, it's good practice."

"Right," Maggie said. "And it's in the hospital. How scary can that be?"

Chapter Thirteen

The three adults waited silently downstairs until they heard the door to Clarissa's room close. Then Mary turned to her mother. "Mom, have I ever mentioned Mike, Clarissa's guardian angel?" she asked casually as she walked back to the kitchen followed by Margaret and Bradley.

"He's the fireman, isn't he?" Margaret asked. "His parents came to the baby shower."

Mary nodded. "Exactly," she said. "He's a pretty important member of our family. And you're going to get the chance to meet him."

She stopped next to the kitchen counter and called, "Mike, are you around?"

Instantly Mike appeared next to her. "Good morning," he said. Then he turned and looked at Margaret, who was staring at him in shock. "Hi, Mom."

"Hello," Margaret replied slowly, still surprised.

Mike nodded. "I know, you don't often see a such a good-looking guy like me," he said with a dramatic sigh. "I have that effect on most women."

Margaret's face softened, and she chuckled. "Do you now?" she asked. "And being so modest, it must be a chore."

Laughing, Mike nodded. "Exactly," he teased. Then he turned to Mary. "Mary, your mother is not only beautiful, she's highly intelligent."

"How can I see you?" Margaret asked.

"Well, I want you to see me," Mike explained, turning back to Margaret. "So that's part. But also, you are connected to this family, and so that helps too."

Then he looked back over at Mary. "What's up?"

"That's the question of the hour," Mary said.

Bradley nodded. "Yeah, something's up with Clarissa and Maggie."

"What?" Margaret asked. "Why would you say that?"

Bradley laughed. "My daughter is good, but she's not that good," he said.

"And when she couldn't meet our eyes when we complimented her," Mary added. "That's a sure sign that she's feeling guilty about something."

"And her movements— shuffling her feet, lowering her head," Bradley added. "All physiological signs of internal stress, which comes from lying."

"That's what you get for having two trained law enforcement professionals as parents," Mike inserted. "You never get away with stuff."

"This is amazing," Margaret said. "I should have been trained like this when you were young."

Mary shook her head. "No, you had Mom Radar," she said. "You would know when we did something wrong even if we were miles away from home. You didn't need training."

Margaret shook her head. "Obviously, from our Halloween conversations, the Mom Radar didn't work all the time."

"Thank goodness," Mary laughed. Then she looked at Mike. "So, what do you know?"

Mike shook his head. "Okay, you know the rules," he said. "I'm here to watch over her, not come running to you guys if she makes a bad decision. She has the freedom to choose, too."

"Well, technically, you didn't come to us," Bradley said, "because we already figured out that something was up. But, you could help us with some insight so we can figure out how far we let her take her decision making."

"Fair enough," Mike said with a nod. "Well, she might have overheard your conversation about the ghost children last night. And, to give her credit, she was going to come downstairs until she overheard Bradley asking all of you not to mention it to her."

"Ahhhh," Bradley said slowly. "Okay, that makes sense. Do you have an idea of what her plan might be?"

Mike smiled and nodded. "She might have called Maggie with a walkie-talkie she has stashed in her bedroom and said something about going to the hospital to see Stanley and then asking to go to the bathroom," Mike offered. "Then they might have decided to take the elevator down to three and check it out."

"Well, that's brilliant," Mary said, impressed with their deviousness. "What do you think?"

"No," Bradley said immediately. "It's too dangerous."

Margaret smiled at him. He was such a good father.

"Actually," Mike offered, "there is no danger from the children, and Clarissa and Maggie might be just who we need to get them to trust us."

Bradley shook his head. "I don't like it." He looked at Mary. "What do you think?"

Mary was torn. She didn't like the idea of Clarissa and Maggie walking around in that dark hallway, being spooked. But maybe being spooked would prevent them from taking other, more dangerous, risks in the future.

"Well, I understand what you're feeling," she said. "I was pretty spooked when we were on that floor. But this might be a good learning experience for the girls. And it will be a controlled experience."

Mike nodded. "I'll be there with them," he said.

"And once they leave to go to the bathroom, I can follow them," Margaret offered.

Sighing, Bradley leaned back against the kitchen wall. "Okay," he said. "But let me do a little research this morning on the file we found. If I find anything that makes me uncomfortable, we call this off."

"Agreed," Mary said. "And I'll see what I can find on my end. Mom, we'll call you by eleven to update you."

Margaret nodded. "That's perfect," she said, grinning. "This is quite exciting, you know. I've never been part of a case before."

Mary laughed. "Who knows? This might be the start of a whole new career for you."

Margaret shook her head. "Well, I don't know about that," she said. "But I'm sure this will be an adventure for all of us."

Chapter Fourteen

"Well, what do we have here?" Stanley asked when Margaret and the girls came into his hospital room. "Have the angels come to take me away?"

Maggie and Clarissa giggled.

"Hello, Stanley," Margaret said. "The girls had the day off school and wanted to pay you a visit. I hope that's okay."

"Darn tootin it's okay," Stanley said. "I've been so bored I started counting the number of tiles on the floor."

Clarissa looked down at the tiny ceramic floor tiles beneath her. "Wow, you were bored," she said. "My mom said she beat you in poker."

Margaret bit back a grin and covered her laughter with a cough, but Stanley glanced in her direction with a smile in his eyes. "Well, iffen you can keep a secret," he said, "I guess I can let you know that I let her win."

"You did?" Maggie asked. "Why?"

"Well, you know, she is expecting and all," he replied. "So, I didn't want to do nothing that would upset that there baby."

"Would losing at poker upset the baby?" Clarissa asked Margaret.

Seeing the real concern on Clarissa's face, Margaret shook her head. "I am pretty sure your mom could handle losing a couple of card games," she said. "But it was lovely of Stanley to consider her feelings."

Stanley blushed slightly. "Yeah, well, I ain't called Stanley the Gentleman fer nothing," he said.

"I've never heard you called that," Maggie said.

"Me either," Clarissa added.

"Well, you ain't always around me, right?" Stanley asked. "Could be people call me stuff you ain't ever even heard about."

"Like what?" Maggie asked.

Stanley shook his head. "What do you mean, like what?"

"Like what other names do people call you?" she replied.

Chuckling softly, Margaret sat in a chair and folded her arms, waiting for his response. "Well?" she prompted. "What do they call you?"

Stanley harrumphed loudly and sat back against the pile of pillows on his bed. "Well, I ain't the kind of man to brag," he said.

"Then they must call you Stanley the Modest," Margaret supplied.

"Yeah!" Clarissa agreed. "And Stanley the Brave 'cause of how you saved Rosie when your house was on fire."

"And Stanley the Sick 'cause you're in the hospital," Maggie suggested.

Margaret laughed out loud. "Stanley the Sick does have a nice ring to it," she teased.

Stanley laughed too. "No. No. Them's all too ordinary," he said. "How about Stanley the Superstar?"

"Oh, that's a good one," Clarissa said. "Do they really call you that?"

Stanley chuckled. "Nope, they never have," he laughed. "But I'm hoping they do some day."

"We made you some get well cards," Maggie said. "We can put superstar on them if you'd like."

Stanley's eyes softened, and he shook his head. "Well, ain't that the sweetest thing," he said, his voice a little hoarse. "No, you don't need to put superstar on them. I feel like a superstar just getting them."

They brought over their cards, bedazzled with glitter and colored markers, and gave them to him. Stanley studied them for several minutes and then looked up at the girls, his eyes moist. "These are the most beautiful cards I've ever gotten in my whole life," he said. "I will treasure them always."

Clarissa shrugged. "They're really not that great," she pointed out frankly. "We kind of made them in a hurry. But we can make you better ones if you want."

He smiled at them. "Well, I still want to keep these," he said. "But I would sure like getting more cards from you."

"Okay," Maggie said. "We can make you a card every week. Then you'll really feel like a superstar."

"I really will," Stanley agreed.

Just then, Margaret's phone buzzed. She looked down to see that she had a text message from Mary. *"Bradley says everything's okay. Enjoy the adventure."*

"Who was that?" Clarissa asked.

"That was your mom," Margaret replied, "telling us to enjoy our adventure."

The girls shared furtive glances with each other and then Clarissa met Margaret's eyes. "Um, Grandma, can I go to the bathroom please?" she asked.

"Oh, me too," Maggie added. "I have to go really bad."

"Well, I got a bathroom right here in this room," Stanley said. "You can use that iffen you'd like."

Clarissa shook her head. "Oh, no, we don't want to do that," she said. "That would be…um…imposing. We can just go down the hall. Okay?"

"Well, I don't know," Margaret replied. "This is a public building."

"We'll be safe, I promise," Clarissa begged. "We won't be long either. And we'll stay together."

"We promise," Maggie added.

Margaret sighed. "Well, I suppose so," she said, trying hard not to smile. "But hurry back."

"We will," Clarissa said, grabbing Maggie's hand and running to the door. "We'll be right back."

Chapter Fifteen

Clarissa and Maggie hurried down the hall towards the elevator then stopped together in front of the doors.

"Should we really do this?" Maggie asked.

Clarissa stared at the shiny, stainless-steel doors in front of her and took a deep breath. "If we can't do it now, how can we do it when we're grown up?" she asked, still staring straight ahead.

"But when we're grown up, we'll be older," Maggie replied. "And it won't be as scary."

Clarissa shook her head. "Even my mom and dad were scared," she said.

Maggie looked at her. "They were?" she asked, her eyes widening. "You didn't tell me that."

Clarissa turned and looked at her friend. "I didn't want you to be too scared to go," she admitted.

"I think I am too scared," Maggie said, shaking her head.

"Okay, let's just take the elevator and see, okay?" Clarissa pleaded. "If it's too scary, we can come right back up here."

Maggie looked at the elevator doors and then back at Clarissa. "Okay," she said with a sigh. "We can go down there and see. But—"

"If it's too scary," Clarissa inserted. "Yeah, I know."

She stepped forward, pressed the down button, and the elevator doors opened immediately. Both girls swallowed audibly, grabbed each other's hands, and stepped forward into the empty elevator. The door closed behind them, and they took a deep breath. No sooner had they released that last breath than the doors opened again.

The lobby in front of them was dim, and a flickering fluorescent light gave the shadows movement. Still holding hands, Clarissa and Maggie stepped forward onto the floor and looked around.

"We're supposed to go through those doors," Clarissa whispered, pointing past the nurses station.

"Why are we whispering?" Maggie whispered.

Clarissa turned to Maggie and a nervous giggle escaped her lips. "I don't know," she giggled. "In case the ghosts are sleeping."

Maggie giggled too. "Do ghosts sleep?"

"I don't know," Clarissa replied and then, instead of a giggle, she snorted. She immediately clapped her hand over her mouth and turned to Maggie. Maggie's nervous giggles turned to laughter. And it was contagious. In a few moments both girls were laughing so hard, there were tears running down their cheeks.

"What's so funny?"

Maggie stopped laughing immediately and turned towards the voice.

"What?" Clarissa asked, instantly aware of Maggie's movement.

Maggie reached back and grabbed Clarissa's hand, so both of them could see the little girl standing next to the nurses station.

"What's so funny?" the young girl repeated.

"Clarissa snorted," Maggie said.

The ghost's lips turned upward. "That's all?" she asked.

"It was pretty loud," Clarissa admitted. "It kind of echoed."

The ghost's laughter rang through the room. "That is funny," she said. "Do you want to meet my friends?"

The girls glanced at each other and then turned back to the ghost. "Sure," Clarissa said. "But we can't be too long."

"We're supposed to be going to the bathroom," Maggie admitted.

"You snuck away?" the ghost asked, excitement tinging her voice.

Clarissa nodded. "Yeah, it was pretty easy," she said.

The ghost smiled. "I like you," she said. "I like you a lot."

Chapter Sixteen

The hallway beyond the swinging doors was even darker than the one just outside the elevator. Maggie and Clarissa continued to hold hands for support as they followed the little ghost girl who glided up the hallway in front of them.

"Are your friends close by?" Clarissa asked.

The ghost looked back over her shoulder and smiled. "Uh-huh," she said. "Back here in the special place."

They were nearing the end of the hall, and Maggie looked around. "But, there are no more rooms left," she said, confused.

The little girl nodded. "That's what they wanted people to think," she said. "But there's more. Just a little bit further."

Just beyond the last room, the ghost turned to the right, into a small alcove and the same door that Bradley and Mary had seen the night before was in front of them.

"Wow, I would have never guessed this was back here," Clarissa said.

The door slowly opened toward them and they both caught their breath. Then, they could see the little boy pushing the door open from the other side.

"This is Jack," the little girl said. "He's usually on guard duty."

"Guard duty?" Maggie asked.

"So the bad people can't get to us anymore," the little ghost replied.

"I'm Clarissa," Clarissa said. "And this is Maggie. We didn't get introduced earlier."

The ghost smiled. "Sorry, I'm Anna," she said. "I'm the oldest of the gang, so I always check things out."

"I'm nine," Clarissa said. "How old are you?"

"I'm eight," Anna replied. "And Jack's six."

"Are there a lot more kids?" Maggie asked.

Anna nodded her head. "Yeah, there are thirteen of us," she said sadly. "The doctor used to call us his baker's dozen."

"The doctor?" Clarissa asked. "Was he trying to get you better?"

Anna thought about that for a long moment. "I think so," she said. "That's what he told us." She sighed, then looked up and smiled, brushing the sadness away. "You want to meet the other kids?"

"Sure," Clarissa said. "That would be great."

They followed Jack and when the door closed solidly behind them, they both jumped. Anna laughed. "Scaredy-cats!"

Maggie laughed half-heartedly. "Yeah, I guess so."

There were windows on their left, but they were darkened with dirt and only seemed to look out onto a brick wall. The corridor was narrow, and the rooms on the right side were tiny, only big enough for a small bed and a table. Each room had an adjoining bath with a minuscule shower, sink and toilet.

"They're all kid sized," Anna explained. "That's what they told us."

About half-way down the corridor was a nurses station with television monitors at the desk and a room behind it.

"That's where they put the medicines," Jack said as he rubbed his tiny arm. "Medicines hurt."

Clarissa nodded. "I know," she said. "I hate shots. Did you have to get shots?"

"Lots," Jack said. "Lots and lots."

Maggie released Clarissa's hand and walked behind the nurses station. The countertops were empty except for a thick layer of dust. She pulled open a drawer to find a couple of pencils, a pen and some rubberbands. "There's not much left here," she said to Anna.

Anna shook her head. "No, one day they all left," she said. "No one ever came back."

"They left you here?" Maggie asked, shocked. "They just left you?"

"Maggie," Clarissa called. "I can't see anything anymore."

Maggie began to hurry back around the counter when she saw a ring of keys hanging from a small hook underneath the top counter. She quickly grabbed them and pushed them in her pocket. She reached over and took Clarissa's hand.

Suddenly the hall was filled with other ghost children, all wearing hospital gowns. Their eyes were shadowed, and their faces were drawn. All of them were thin, and some had purpling bruises on their arms.

Clarissa's heart jumped at the sudden onslaught of so many ghosts.

"Are these your friends?" Maggie asked, her voice shaking slightly.

Anna nodded. "And we haven't had new friends for a long time," she said. "We want you to be our friends."

Taking a deep breath, Clarissa tried to smile at Anna. "Well, we would like to," she explained. "But, like I said, we can't stay very long."

Anna shook her head. "If you want, you can stay forever."

Chapter Seventeen

Margaret paced in front of the elevator on the fourth floor, stopping every few moment and checking her phone. Those girls had been gone for over twenty minutes and she was feeling more than a little nervous about the whole situation.

She glanced back at her phone again and made a decision. She accessed her message application and texted Mary. *Girls still not back after 20 minutes. Should I go down?*

She pressed send and waited. And waited. And waited.

Three minutes had passed. An eternity. What was Mary doing? Maybe she hadn't seen it.

She copied and pasted the text and sent it again.

Tapping her foot impatiently she looked up at the elevator's lights, willing it to light up and have the girls walk out. She looked down at her text, still unanswered.

"That's it," she said aloud and stepped forward to press the down button. Nothing happened. She pressed it again still no electronic response. She hurried back to the nurses station.

"Hello!" she called. "The elevator's not working."

"Oh, not again," the nurse replied with a smile. "That one is always offline."

"What?" Margaret asked, panic shooting through her. "Well, I have to get downstairs. Right away."

"Sure," the nurse replied, pointing in the opposite direction. "There's another elevator around the corner."

"Does it go down to the third floor?" Margaret asked.

The nurse shook her head. "No, but that really doesn't matter because the third floor on this side of the hospital is under construction."

Margaret took a shaky breath and nodded. "But what about the other side of the third floor?" she asked. "The part that isn't under construction?"

"Oh, well, you would actually need to go back down to the first floor and then back to the main lobby and use that bank of elevators," she said with a wince of apology. "I'm sorry for the inconvenience."

"The stairs," Margaret suggested. "Can I use the stairs to access the third floor?"

The nurse nodded and then shrugged. "Well, yes, in the wing that's open," she said. "But the door to the area under renovation is locked. You know, for security reasons."

Margaret nodded, trying to present a calm façade that she didn't feel. "And how often do these elevators stop working like this?" she asked.

"Lately they've been really bad," the nurse replied. "I'll call them right away to get someone on it."

"Well, thank you," Margaret asked. She hurried down the hall towards the original elevator and the staircase. Lock or no lock, she was going to get onto that third floor.

Chapter Eighteen

Mary looked through the packages of thick slab bacon and finally decided on the one she wanted. The small butcher shop in Lena only carried locally raised meat, and Mary's mom had raved about the taste of the bacon the last time she visited. The only problem was that the old brick building that lay in the shadow of the water tower had absolutely no cell service. But, Mary decided, with the girls under her mother's care and Mike as a backup, she would have no problem running the twenty-minute errand from her office to the butcher shop.

She picked up one more package of bacon and then looked at the other fresh meat and deli selections offered. She thought about the menu for the upcoming week and selected several more items before placing her basket on the checkout counter.

"I'll be with you in a minute," the owner called from the adjoining office. "I'm just taking a meat order."

"No problem," Mary said. "I have plenty of time."

She automatically pulled out her phone and looked at it, then shook her head when she saw there were no new messages or emails. "Duh, Mary," she whispered to herself. "No bars, no information."

She casually flipped through recipe cards displayed on the counter and decided a couple of them looked like something she'd like to try.

"Oh, you can take those recipes if you'd like," the owner said, coming up to the cash register.

"Really? Thank you. They look great," Mary replied.

"I tried the stew last week," the owner said. "It was great. But if you really want to change it up a little, I can give you a couple of tips."

Knowing her limited epicurean skills, Mary nodded eagerly. "I would really like that," she said.

The woman looked at her and finally said, "When I was in my last months of pregnancy my mind was like a sieve. Would you like me to write it down?"

Grinning, Mary nodded. "I would love that," she said. "My friend told me about pregnancy brain and I'm so glad she did. I thought I was totally losing it."

The owner laughed and nodded. "I'll be right back. Let me just run to the office for paper and a pen."

Chapter Nineteen

"We can't stay forever," Maggie replied. "We have to go to school tomorrow."

"I used to go to school," Jack said, floating up next to them. "Before I got sick."

"That's so sad, Jack," Clarissa replied. "What was your favorite class?"

Jack smiled shyly at Clarissa. "I liked art," he replied. "Especially finger-painting."

"I bet you were good at it," Clarissa said.

"If you stayed with us, you wouldn't have to go to school," Anna suggested.

Maggie looked around them. All of the ghosts were forming a semi-circle that blocked them against the wall. She started to feel a little nervous about the situation. But all of the ghosts were smiling at them. That was a good thing. Right?

"What happened to your families?" Clarissa asked.

Suddenly the faces of the children changed. They were no longer happy and open. They were angry.

"We don't have families," Anna said defiantly. "And we don't need them."

"Families are stupid," Jack shouted. "Stupid. Stupid. Stupid."

"No, they're not," Clarissa argued.

Maggie squeezed her hand. "Don't argue," she whispered frantically. "Don't make them angry."

Suddenly all of the doors started to slam shut, one after the other, the sharp blasts echoing off the walls.

"What's that?" Clarissa asked.

"We don't need families," Anna said. "We just need new friends."

"Crap," Maggie whispered. "This is not good."

"We can be your friends," Clarissa said, trying to be calm. "But we just can't stay here with you."

Anna shook her head. "You can't leave," she replied.

"I thought you said you were our friend?" Clarissa replied. "Friends aren't mean to other friends."

"You lied to me," Anna said. "You didn't want to be our friends. You lied to us."

"Lied to us," one of the other ghosts repeated. "Lied to us."

"Lied to us," another one whispered. "Lied. Lied. Lied."

"This is so not good," Maggie said, her heart pounding. "We need to get out of here."

Clarissa looked at the ghost children who were all chanting now. "I need to tell them about the light," she whispered to Maggie.

"Do they look like they want to listen to you right now?" Maggie replied.

Looking back, Clarissa saw the anger and the determination in their eyes. She shook her head. "No, they look like they want to hurt us," she said.

"Or keep us here. Forever," Maggie said, her voice trembling. "What should we do?"

"Mike!" Clarissa called out. "Mike, can you help me?"

A soft, glowing light appeared at the end of the hall and slowly made its way towards the group. Jack saw it first. "Look," he said pointing. "What's that?"

The ghost children turned and watched as the light intensified as it got closer to them.

"It's the doctor," one of the children screamed. "He's back!"

Clarissa shook her head and turned to Anna. "No, it's not..." she began.

With translucent tears running down her cheeks, Anna looked at Clarissa. "Run," she whispered, her voice trembling. "Run away before he gets you too."

She disappeared, and a moment later all of the ghost children were gone.

The light slowly dimmed until they could see Mike leaning against the wall and shaking his head. "You two have a lot of explaining to do," he said.

Clarissa and Maggie ran forward to throw their arms around Mike, but they just ran through him. They quickly turned around, their eyes filled with tears. Mike shook his head sympathetically. "Here, let's try this," he said.

A warm light emanated from Mike and swept over the girls. It felt just like a warm hug, filling their hearts with peace. "How's that?" he asked kindly.

"Better," Maggie said, sniffing back her tears. "We were pretty scared."

He nodded. "Yeah, I could see that. Come on, let's get you back upstairs."

They walked to the door, and Clarissa pulled it open. "We just wanted to help," Clarissa added. "We thought they'd talk to kids."

The door closed behind them, and they continued up the dim, empty hallway.

Mike nodded. "And you were right. They did talk to you," he agreed. "But, you know, maybe lying to do a good deed isn't the best way to go about it."

Maggie and Clarissa both nodded.

"Thank you for saving us," Clarissa said a moment later, then she paused. "You don't have to tell on us, right?"

Suddenly, they could hear a loud pounding sound coming from the lobby area. Mike looked up and grinned.

"I have a feeling that I won't have to tell on you," he said.

Chapter Twenty

Mike hurried the girls out to the lobby, the pounding increasing.

"It's coming from the door," Maggie said. "Don't open it."

Mike shook his head. "It's your grandmother," he explained. "You'd better open it."

Clarissa gasped and then flew across the lobby to the door, pulling it open so quickly that Margaret nearly fell forward. "Are you okay?" Margaret breathed. "You had me worried sick!"

"Grandma," Clarissa cried, burying herself in her grandmother's embrace.

Margaret hugged Clarissa and then looked up to see Maggie standing only a few feet away, silent tears coursing down her cheeks. "Come here, darling," she invited.

She didn't have to ask twice. Maggie threw herself into Margaret's arms, crying just as intensely as Clarissa. "Well, there there, darlings," Margaret soothed. "It's all right now. You're safe. You're fine now."

The sobs lessened to sniffles, and a few moments later, Clarissa stepped back to face her grandmother. "I lied, Grandma," she stuttered, wiping the moisture from her cheeks with her sleeve. "I didn't ask to come to the hospital to see Grandpa Stanley. I came to see the ghosts."

"Ah," Margaret replied slowly. "And why would you lie to me?"

"Because I didn't think anyone would let us go, just me and Maggie," she replied with a slow, shuddering breath.

"And now, after your experience, can you understand why your parents might not have wanted to let you go? Just you and Maggie?" she asked.

Maggie looked up, her eyes red-rimmed and her skin blotchy. "They didn't want to let us leave," she said, her eyes wide with fright. "They wanted us to stay with them forever."

Clarissa nodded. "If Mike hadn't come..." she began, and then she stopped and shook her head.

"Aye, but Mike did come," Margaret said, enfolding them both again. "And he did save you. And you've learned a valuable lesson, I hope."

Clarissa nodded.

"And what would that be?" Margaret asked.

"Don't be stupid," she said earnestly.

Margaret bit back a smile and winked at Mike, who was having a hard time containing his own laughter. "And that's a fine lesson, it is," Margaret said. "But not all you did was stupid."

"We talked to the ghosts," Maggie suggested. "We found out there are thirteen of them."

"Thirteen!" Margaret exclaimed. "So many lost children."

"Grandma, do we have to tell…" Clarissa began, but before she could finish the door flew open and Bradley rushed in.

"Clarissa!" he exclaimed. "Maggie. Are you okay?"

They both nodded, and Bradley leaned back against the wall. "I've never run up stairs so fast in my life," he breathed. He turned to Margaret. "Mary got your text and tried to call you, but you didn't pick up. So, she called me."

"I didn't have service in the stairwell," Margaret said.

"How did you get in?" Bradley asked.

"We opened it for her," Clarissa said. "She was pounding on the door like she was going to break it."

Margaret nodded. "And I would have if you hadn't answered soon," she said firmly. She turned to Bradley. "How did you get in?"

He held up a key. "Maintenance key," he said. "He didn't argue when I asked him for it. I don't know if it was the wild look in my eyes or my gun."

Margaret chuckled. "Well, if you looked at all like you did when you burst in here, it was the look."

"Let me call Mary and let her know you're all okay," he said, pulling out his phone. He glanced at Clarissa and Maggie. "And then we'll have a conversation with the two of you."

Chapter Twenty-one

Mary took a deep breath before she opened the front door. She knew she had to pull herself together emotionally before she faced Clarissa and Maggie. She had been frightened to death when she finally saw her mother's text as she walked out of the butcher shop, frightened, and then filled with guilt. What had they been thinking?

They knew the girls were going to do this, and they allowed it! How could they have decided that it was a good idea?

She took another breath and readjusted the grocery bags she was carrying. She needed to be calm and clear-headed when she walked in. They had been frightened enough. They didn't need her freaking out.

Opening the door, she walked in and saw the girls sitting side by side on the couch. She put the bags on the floor and immediately walked over to them. "How are you doing?" she asked.

Clarissa looked up at her, her eyes moist with tears. "Are you disappointed with me?" she asked softly.

Mary sighed and pulled Clarissa into her arms. "Darling, I am too relieved that you're okay to even think about being disappointed," she admitted.

She reached over and pulled Maggie into the hug. "Are you okay?"

Both girls hugged her back in silence. They stayed that way for several minutes until Mary finally stepped back. "Okay, we need to have a family discussion about this," she said.

Both girls nodded.

"I'm going to run upstairs and change," Mary said. "And perhaps we can order some pizza and then have a chat. Okay?"

"Okay," Clarissa agreed, still looking hesitant.

"I guess," Maggie said.

Mary looked at Maggie. "Should I call your parents and let them know what happened?"

Maggie's eyes grew round. "Can we wait?" she asked. "You know, until after we all talk?"

Mary nodded. "Okay, we can wait," she agreed. "I'll be down in a few minutes."

She picked up the bags and brought them into the kitchen. Bradley and Margaret were standing in the kitchen, waiting for her. Bradley took the bags and peeked inside. "Bacon?" he asked with a smile. "You bought bacon."

Mary shook her head. "That bacon nearly cost me and my mother a heart attack," she replied.

"Well, what do you want to do next?" Margaret asked.

Mary turned to her mother. "Wait, you're the adult with the most experience here," she said. "Shouldn't you be in charge?"

Margaret smiled but shook her head. "This is out of my experience base," she said. "But I think we need to have an atmosphere that calms their hearts and encourages discussion, rather than one that chastises."

"I agree," Mary said. "I was thinking a family discussion with pizza." She looked at Bradley. "Could you order some?"

He nodded. "And I'm thinking some cannoli would be appropriate for the occasion," he suggested with a smile.

"Cannoli is always appropriate for any occasion," Mary replied. "I'm going to run up and get changed. Then we can meet."

She hurried up the stairs to her bedroom and immediately kicked off her shoes. Then, after going to the bathroom, she changed into loose sweat pants and a sweat shirt and felt like a new person. She pulled on thick wool socks and started to head back down stairs when she heard a sound from Clarissa's bedroom. Moving as quietly as possible, she approached the door and listened. Was it just Lucky, their kitten? She put her ear against the door. No, definitely not.

Slowly opening the door, Mary looked inside. In the corner of the room was the ghost of a little boy, sitting on the floor, his arms around his knees, crying.

Mary slipped inside and sat on the bed.

112

"Hi," she said softly, hoping not to frighten him.

He looked up at her, his eyes filled with fear. "Are you going to hurt me?" he whispered.

She shook her head. "No, I would never hurt you," she said. "Has someone else hurt you?"

"The doctor," he whispered, glancing around in terror. "The doctor hurt me."

"Which doctor?" Mary asked.

"The one with the shots," the boy replied.

"Oh, I hate shots," she said emphatically.

The boy nodded. "Me too," he said. "I hate them lots!"

"What's your name?" Mary asked.

The boy stared at her for a long moment and then sighed. "Jack," he finally replied. "I'm Jack."

"Hi Jack," she said with a tender smile. "I'm Mary.

"Are you Clarissa's friend?" he asked.

Mary nodded. Ah, well that made sense. Jack must have been one of the children at the hospital and he connected himself to Clarissa. "Yes, I'm Clarissa's mom," she replied. "Clarissa's downstairs. Do you want to come down?"

He shook his head. "No, I'll just stay here for now."

"Okay," Mary said. "You're safe here, Jack."

Jack looked up at her and smiled tremulously. "Thank you," he said. Then he faded from view.

Chapter Twenty-two

Mary came downstairs and found everyone sitting around the table. Even Mike had pulled up a chair and was floating above it.

"Sorry I took so long," Mary said, seating herself. "I just had a conversation with Jack."

Maggie and Clarissa started and turned to Mary. "Jack's here?" Clarissa asked.

Mary nodded. "I heard him crying and found him in your bedroom," she replied.

"Poor Jack," Maggie said. "I think he was the littlest. He told us he was six."

Mary sighed. "Okay, we need to discuss what happened today," she said. "And we need you to be honest about your feelings, okay?"

The girls nodded in unison.

Mary turned to Clarissa. "Why don't you start," she suggested.

Clarissa nodded. "I got up to go to the bathroom last night, and I heard you talking downstairs," she said. "I heard you talking about the ghost girl and how she was afraid of you. And I thought that she probably wouldn't be afraid of another kid, so Maggie and I could help."

Clarissa turned to Bradley. "Then you said that you shouldn't talk about it to us because it might frighten us," she admitted. "So, I knew you probably wouldn't agree to let us help you."

Bradley nodded. "Well, at that point, you were probably right," he agreed. "But I think I would have been willing to discuss it."

She dropped her head and nodded. Then she looked back up at him. "I was afraid to ask permission," she said. "Because you might say no."

Margaret glanced over at Mary and lifted her eyebrows pointedly. Mary agreed silently. That sounded exactly like something she would do.

"What did you do next?" Mary asked.

Clarissa glanced over at Maggie, then back to Mary. "I called Maggie on our walkie-talkies, and we made a plan to go to the hospital with Grandma," she continued.

"So, you didn't really want to see Grandpa Stanley?" Bradley asked.

"We did," Clarissa reasoned. "Just not for very long."

"Actually, they did have a short visit with Stanley," Margaret inserted. "And they made him two very nice get-well cards."

"Then we said we had to go to the bathroom, and we went downstairs to the third floor," Clarissa finished.

"Where you frightened?" Mike asked.

Both girls nodded. "We didn't really want to go at first," Maggie said.

"Why did you go?" Mike asked.

"Because we thought we could help the little girl ghost," Clarissa said. "Sometimes when you're helping someone you have to do scary things."

Mary smiled. "That's true," she said. "And it was very brave of you to go down there." She studied the girls. "So, can both of you see ghosts?"

"Only when Clarissa holds my hand," Maggie said. "Then she can see them too."

"What happened when you got to the third floor?" Bradley asked.

"We were so scared that we started giggling," Clarissa said. "And the little girl ghost wanted to know why we were laughing. Then she took us to meet the other ones."

"How many others?" Mary asked.

"Thirteen ghosts," Maggie said. "They said the doctor called them his baker's dozen."

"They said everyone left them there," Clarissa added. "The doctors and nurses just left them there and locked up the special hallway."

"Just left them there?" Margaret asked, appalled. "Who would do such a thing?"

Mary turned to her mother. "Well, it could be that they had all died," she explained. "But if they didn't realize it, they could have felt like they were just left there."

"The special hallway was creepy," Maggie said. "It looked like they just moved out quickly. They left all kinds of stuff by the nurses station."

"I bet there are files in there," Bradley said, shaking his head. "I asked the maintenance man about the hall, and he said there were no keys to get in there anymore. So, we can't even access them if they were left behind."

Maggie reached into her pocket and pulled out the keys she found at the nurses station. "Maybe these will help," she said. "I found them when we were there."

Chapter Twenty-three

The girls had just finished recounting their experiences on the third floor when the doorbell rang. Everyone at the table jumped at the sound, which caused a round of slightly embarrassed laughter.

Bradley answered the door, paid for the pizza and set it in the middle of the table. "Why don't we all fill our plates before we continue," he suggested.

He opened the box, and the aroma filled the room. It didn't take long before everyone had a steaming slice of cheesy pizza on their plates.

"So, now that we've passed out the pizza," Bradley said to Maggie and Clarissa, "let's talk about how you two are feeling about your experience."

Clarissa stopped mid-bite and looked at him. "Our experience?" she asked.

Mary nodded. "How are you feeling about meeting all those ghosts and then thinking you were going to be trapped with them?" she asked.

Maggie put her pizza down on her plate and looked over at Mary and Bradley. "I was afraid at first, when we got there," she explained. "Then, when I met Jack and Anna, I was okay. They were just kids. But when all the other kids came, and they wanted us to stay, I was scared. I didn't know if they could make us stay or if they could hurt us."

"I bet that was scary," Mary agreed. "There were a lot of ghosts surrounding you."

Clarissa nodded. "And they were angry too," she said. "When we said we couldn't stay, they thought we were lying to them."

"Did you lie to them?" Mary asked.

The girls both shook their heads. "No, we didn't," Maggie said. "We told Anna that we couldn't stay very long."

"Right," Mary said. "Why do you think they got angry?"

The girls thought about it for a few minutes. Finally, Clarissa responded. "It sounds like other people lied to them and hurt them," Clarissa said. "They're afraid of the doctor coming back. They thought Mike was the doctor."

Maggie nodded. "They all ran away when they saw his light coming down the hall," she added.

"How did that make you feel?" Mary asked. "When Mike was coming to help."

"I felt like I could breathe again," Maggie said. "I was so scared just before that. But when Mike came, I thought that everything was going to be fine."

"What would you have done if Mike hadn't come?" Bradley asked.

Clarissa shook her head slowly. "I don't know," she said softly. She turned to Maggie. "Maybe we would have run?"

Maggie shrugged. "I was so scared. I don't know if my legs would have worked," she admitted. "I don't know what I would have done."

Mary nodded. "I'm not sure I could have run if I were in your shoes," she admitted. She paused for a moment and studied both of the girls sitting across from her. "Now, if you could go back and change things, what would you do differently?"

"Even though I was scared," Clarissa said, "I don't know if I would change things." She glanced over at Bradley. "I probably should have asked permission."

He nodded. "Yes, you probably should have."

"But what we wanted to do," she replied emphatically, "we did. We found out about the ghost children. We talked to them. We learned stuff. Important stuff."

"I think Clarissa's right," Maggie said. "Even though it was really scary and next time I'd want someone there to help us, we did what we wanted to do. We talked to them. We learned that they were afraid of the doctor."

"But you put yourselves in danger," Bradley pointed out.

Maggie nodded. "But next time we won't have to lie because you'll know we can handle it."

Mike choked on his laughter and turned away from the table, but not before Bradley saw the amusement in his eyes.

"I'm not sure I know you two can handle it," Bradley replied.

Clarissa turned to Maggie and then looked at her dad. "We can," she said with confidence. "We're just not used to it yet. Just like the first time you saw a ghost. But we know we have to be more careful next time."

"There isn't going to be—" Bradley began.

Mary placed her hand on top of his arm before he could finish his sentence, and he turned to her. "I'm sorry for interrupting," she said. "But could you help me with something for a moment?"

Nodding, he stood up and followed Mary into the privacy of the living room.

"I don't want them doing something like this again," he whispered vehemently.

She nodded. "I totally agree with you," she said.

His jaw dropped for a moment. "Wait. You put your hand on my arm," he said. "That normally means 'Shut up, Bradley. You're going to say something dumb.'"

124

"No," she denied emphatically. "You never say anything dumb. But sometimes I want you to consider another perspective before you continue. That's all."

He smiled at her. "Well, that certainly sounds better than dumb," he teased. "What do you want me to consider?"

Mary stepped forward and kissed him, then stepped back. "First, I want you to know that I think I understand your perspective. I understand that the most important thing for you is to protect your family and friends and keep them safe. And I know, without a doubt, that you would do anything to make sure that we are all protected," she began. "And there's absolutely nothing wrong or dumb about that."

He nodded. "Thank you," he replied softly. "I appreciate that."

"So, now here's the but part," she teased.

He laughed. "Okay, I'm ready."

"Clarissa and Maggie have a unique bond," she said. "And with that bond, a unique gift. Together they can do things most people can't."

"Yeah, I get that," he replied.

"And they feel responsible for that gift," she explained. "And, I think, a little pumped that they can do what they do."

"I still don't want them running off and doing it without permission," he said.

"Exactly," Mary replied.

Bradley stared at her for a long moment. "Exactly what?" he asked, suspiciously.

"Exactly, we don't want them running off on their own," she said. "If you forbid them to use their gifts, do you think they're actually going to stop, or are they just not going to tell us because we've forbidden it?"

"Well, if they're obedient, they'll stop," he said.

She paused for a moment, understanding the concern he had for his daughter, the fear he was still feeling from their experience that afternoon. "Okay, let me ask you," she said. "And I want an honest answer."

He nodded.

"You are one of the first responders at the scene of an accident," she began. "A car has rolled over, and you can hear someone crying for help inside the vehicle. It sounds like a child is trapped and can't get out. There is gasoline on the ground, and there's a chance it could catch and the car could go up in flames. The other officer, your superior, tells you to stay back until help arrives, but you know that if you wait for them, it might be too late. What do you do?"

He sighed. "I go for it," he said. "I try and rescue the child."

"Because you're not obedient?" she asked.

"Because I think the consequences outweigh the risks," he replied. "But I'm a professional, and I have been taught how to make those kinds of determinations."

"And the only way Clarissa and Maggie will learn how to make those same kinds of decisions is if we let them continue to do what they want to do, but with limited exposure at this point in their lives," Mary said. "And within the rules we set. So, we don't forbid them to help, but we teach them how to help safely."

He closed his eyes and shook his head. "This is really hard," he whispered to her. "I want to keep her safe, all the time."

Mary wrapped her arms around his waist and leaned her head against his chest. "I know," she said softly. "You are the best father in the world."

He kissed the top of her head. "Okay," he said, taking a deep breath. "Let's go back to the table and figure out the new rules."

She smiled up at him. "If it's any consolation," she said, "we probably need to make sure the Brennans are okay with these rules too."

"Okay, we probably should set up a meeting for tonight," he said, "once we get back from the hospital."

She was surprised. "We're going back to the hospital?" she asked.

"Yeah, I think we need to check out that file room before the evidence disappears."

Chapter Twenty-four

Mary held the flashlight and pointed it toward the lock on the door. But her nerves were taut and her hands shaky, so the beam jumped around. She wasn't sure if she was responding to the fear generated by the ghosts or if her hormones were kicking in again. Bradley was bent in front of her with the keys in hand, trying to put a key into the slot, but the dancing light made it almost impossible.

He turned towards her. "Just a little bit higher," he instructed.

"What?" she asked, shining the light directly into his eyes.

He tried to shield his eyes from the blinding light. "Mary, you're blinding me," he said.

"Oh, sorry," she said, dropping the beam towards the floor. "What did you need?"

"Well, I did need for you to lower the light to the lock," he said dryly. "But, um, now I think I need you to fit the keys into lock while I hold the flashlight because all I can see are big, black spots before my eyes."

Shaking her head, she stepped forward and handed him the flashlight. "Sorry about that," she said.

He leaned forward, kissed her quickly and placed the keys in her hand. "Good thing you're cute," he teased.

She chuckled softly, and the nerves in her stomach loosened. Looking down at the keys, she could see that they all looked alike. "Which one is it?" she asked.

"That's a good question," Bradley replied. "And now you get to find out."

With a determined nod, she moved forward and bent towards the door. "Okay, here goes," she said, picking up the first key. But before she could try and slip it into the lock, the door knob turned, and the door slowly opened.

Remembering what the girls had said about Jack guarding the door, Mary stepped forward and looked down. "Jack?" she questioned gently. "Is that you?"

The little boy appeared before her, bathed in the light of the flashlight. Mary reached back for Bradley's free hand, and once she was holding it, she nodded to Jack. "This is Bradley," she said. "Bradley, this is Jack."

Jack's eyes widened, and he shimmered in the light. "Are you a doctor?" he asked tremulously.

Bradley shook his head. "No, I'm the chief of police," he said. "My job is to protect you."

Jack smiled in wonder. "You'll protect me?" he asked.

Bradley nodded. "Yes, Jack, I will," he said. "You won't have to worry about doctors anymore."

Bradley stepped into the hallway, so the door could close behind them. Then he reached over to a wall switch to try the lights. Half of the fluorescent lights in the long hallway turned outward, casting odd shadows against the walls. But it was better than a single flashlight beam.

"Jack," Mary asked. "Do you know if the room behind the nurses station has files in it? Like the file you slipped through the door the other day?"

Jack nodded. "That's where they kept all the notes," he said. "There's lots of notes in there."

"Okay," Bradley said. "Let's go see."

The little ghost drifted ahead of them in the hallway, almost as if he was skipping. Mary turned to Bradley. "It's amazing, isn't it? He's still just a little boy."

When they reached the nurses station, Jack stopped and turned to them. "It's back there," he said, pointing to the door behind the counter. "The papers and the shots are there."

"Shots?" Mary asked. "What kind of shots?"

"The shots that hurt us," Jack replied.

"Could they have been shots to try to make you better?" Bradley asked.

Jack shook his head slowly. "No, we couldn't get better," he said. "We were too sick."

"Too sick?" Mary asked. "All of you were too sick?"

Jack looked uncomfortable, and he started to fade away.

"Jack," Mary called to him. "We're just trying to help."

"You can't help us," Jack whispered, as he disappeared. "All of us had AIDS."

Chapter Twenty-five

Mary turned to Bradley. "They all had AIDS?" she asked. "Could that be right?"

He pushed a key into the lock and turned it. The door opened before them. "Well, there's one way to find out," he said.

Reaching over, he flipped the wall switch, and the overhead light turned on. The room was the size of a maintenance closet. On one side was a counter with metal cabinets above it. On the other side were a file cabinet and several metal carts for transporting medicine.

Bradley opened a cabinet door and found boxes of old medications in cardboard boxes. "Do we have anything to put these in?" he asked.

"Should we remove them from the hospital?" Mary asked.

He turned to her and sighed, running his hand through his hair. "So, let me give you my take on the situation, and then you can tell me what you think," he said.

"Okay," she said. "Shoot."

"We have a hospital with a hidden unit that has been locked for at least fifteen years," he said. "The maintenance guy knew about it but said in all of his years working here no one has ever opened that door."

Mary nodded. "Okay, that sounds suspicious and creepy," she agreed.

"We've got thirteen kids," he said, "of various ages and gender according to what Clarissa and Maggie saw. And one of them tells us that they all had AIDS."

Mary nodded. "Well, it wasn't that long ago that people didn't understand anything about the HIV virus at all. And mothers were passing it onto their children through childbirth or through nursing. Depending on when the children were patients, it wouldn't be strange to have them isolated."

"Okay, last bit of information," Bradley said, holding up one of the boxes from the cabinet. "All of the boxes are from the same pharmaceutical company, and this one is labeled 'Drug Trial.'"

"Drug Trial?" Mary asked. "As in experimental drugs?"

Bradley nodded. "Exactly."

"This is not looking good," she said. "But, still, the drug company could have donated drugs for the children's care."

"Okay, my final argument," he said. "This section is set for demolition in two weeks. No one was going to pick up files, notes, or these extra canisters of pharmaceuticals. They were all going to be bulldozed and lost forever."

"Yeah, that's the straw that broke this camel's back," Mary agreed. "Let's get the files and some of the drugs."

Mary went out of the room and looked around the area. She found two metal trash containers, dumped out their contents and carried them back into the room. "They aren't fancy," she said.

Bradley smiled. "But they'll work."

Mary moved over to the file cabinet and pulled open the top drawer. Yellowed manila folders filled the top drawers. "I bet you there are twelve files here," she said, pulling them out and counting them as she placed them carefully in the garbage cans. She nodded. "Yep, twelve files."

"Those, with the one at home, make up all thirteen of the children," Bradley agreed. "Anything else in there?"

Mary pulled open the second drawer. A number of notebooks lay in the drawer. She picked up the first one and opened it. "It looks like journal entries," Mary said. "But it looks like medical shorthand, so we're going to need someone with more experience to review them."

She picked them all up and put them in the garbage can alongside the files. "What did you find?" she asked.

"I think I have samples of all of the different kinds of drugs in the cabinets," he said. "So, whoever we find to be our expert will have to let us know about these drugs too."

She slowly looked around the room and then turned to Bradley. "I don't know what we've found," she said, "but it sure seems like these children were victims, not patients. How could that happen?"

Bradley shook his head. "That's exactly what I want to find out."

Chapter Twenty-six

Bradley carried both garbage cans in his arms as they walked down the long hallway toward the elevator. Mary walked ahead of him, shining the flashlight in the dim light. Suddenly Jack appeared before them.

"They're coming," he said. "You have to hide."

"What?" Mary asked Jack.

"What?" Bradley asked Mary.

"They're taking the elevator," Jack said. "Anna saw them. She's the lookout. They know someone's been in the unit."

"Jack said someone's taking the elevator up, and they're looking for us," Mary explained to Bradley. "He wants us to hide."

Bradley looked up and down the hallway. The rooms were stripped bare, and there was no good place to hide. Bradley looked down to where he thought Jack was standing.

"How far away are the men?" Bradley asked.

"They're waiting on the first floor for the elevator," Jack said.

"On the first floor," Mary replied. "Bradley, there's no way we're going to get out of here without them seeing us."

Bradley scanned the area, then noticed an abandoned gurney pushed against a wall in one of the rooms. "Ask Jack if he can open the supply room door," he said. "I need some sheets."

Jack nodded and disappeared.

Bradley put the garbage cans down and pushed the gurney toward Mary. "So, you're just going to go into labor a little early," he said with a smile. He helped her up onto the gurney, and she lay down. Then he slipped the two garbage cans onto the shelves underneath the cart. He looked up and smiled as three sheets seemed to fly down the middle of the hallway on their own.

"Thanks, Jack," he said, taking them from the boy and draping them over Mary and the gurney. "Okay, let's see how good we are at acting."

He quickly pushed Mary out past the double doors and into the lobby just as the elevator doors opened. Three men in dark suits emerged.

"About damn time!" Bradley yelled. "The other elevator stalled on three. She's in transition. Get the hell out of the way!"

Mary moaned loudly, and the men scattered. Bradley pushed the gurney into the elevator and pressed the button to the first floor. Mary moaned again as the door was closing. Then she screamed, "I have to push! I have to push!"

"Breathe!" Bradley ordered as the door finally closed.

The elevator started down, and Mary struggled to sit up. "Okay, I'm breathing," she said with a smile. "Now what?"

He grinned at her. "Lie back down," he said. "This is the fastest way to get us out of the hospital with no questions asked."

She lay back just before the door opened on the first floor. "Should I moan?" she whispered.

He smiled down at her. "No, I think lying there and looking worried is the best bet," he said. "We don't want to draw too much attention to ourselves."

"Well, one thing's for sure," she said as they moved down the corridor on the first floor. "Those guys don't work for the hospital."

"How do you know that?" Bradley asked.

"Because maternity is on two," she said. "There's no reason we would be on three to get to maternity."

"Hopefully they don't figure that out," Bradley replied.

"Why?" Mary asked.

"Because it won't be too hard to figure out who the chief of police and his very pregnant wife are," he said. "And these guys didn't look like part of the construction crew."

Chapter Twenty-seven

"I'm sorry my parents have to tell your parents," Clarissa said to Maggie as they sat together on her bed.

Maggie nodded. "Well, at least it's not as bad as we thought," she replied. "We didn't get punished for sneaking down to the third floor. Well, not yet at least."

"Do you think your parents are going to get mad at you?" Clarissa asked.

Maggie shrugged. "They don't seem to understand things like this like your parents do."

"I think your mom does," Clarissa offered.

"Yeah, but Mom is not too keen on me making up stuff," Maggie said.

"You mean lying?"

Maggie turned to her friend. "Making up stuff sounds lots better than lying."

"You're right," Clarissa said. "It does."

"But this was our first case together," Maggie said. "And that was really cool. I loved being able to see all of those ghosts."

"Yeah, it was pretty cool," Clarissa said.

Maggie smiled. "I felt like a superhero," she added. "You know, like I could see through walls, but really I could see the ghosts."

"I could see them too," Clarissa reminded her.

Maggie shrugged. "Yeah, but only if I touched you," she said, "like I lent you part of my superpowers."

Clarissa turned and stared at her friend for a long moment. Then she slid off the bed and walked over to her desk. "I've been thinking that maybe we should get some equipment," she said.

Maggie followed her to the computer. "What kind of equipment?"

Clarissa jiggled her mouse, and the computer screen came to life. Pictured on the screen was a page filled with paranormal investigation equipment. "Stuff like this," Clarissa said. "So, you know, we could tell when ghosts were around."

145

"But I can see them," Maggie said. "So, we don't need that stuff."

"But all of the real paranormal guys on TV have this stuff," Clarissa argued. "Look, it's an EVP meter. That even sounds cool."

"But the paranormal guys on TV can't really see ghosts," Maggie reiterated. "So, they need it and we don't."

Clarissa turned to her friend. "Maybe you can see them, but I can't," she said.

"You can see them when I touch your hand," Maggie replied.

"But what if I don't always want to touch your hand?" Clarissa asked. "What if I want to figure out if ghosts are there by myself?"

Maggie shook her head and crossed her arms. "That's just silly," she said. "You can either hope that a silly machine picks up their energy or you can just ask me if there's a ghost in the room. I think I'm a little more reliable than a stupid machine."

Clarissa turned in her chair and faced her friend. "Well maybe I don't think they're stupid," she said angrily. "Maybe I think they're cool. Maybe they can pick up things that you and your superpowers can't even see."

"Are you jealous?" Maggie asked, confused.

Clarissa shook her head. "No," she denied. "I'm not. But, you know, since I don't have superpowers like you do, maybe I'm not cool enough to be your friend."

"I didn't say that," Maggie said. "I just said I can see ghosts and you can't."

"I could if I wanted to," Clarissa yelled.

"Could not," Maggie said.

"Well, I can see angels," Clarissa argued.

"Only because you have to have a guardian angel following you around wherever you go," Maggie exclaimed. "Like a big babysitter."

"He is not," Clarissa yelled.

"Right," Maggie said. "You keep believing that."

Clarissa jumped out of her chair and walked across the room, throwing her door wide open. "You can go home now," she said.

"Fine. I wanted to go home anyway," Maggie said, grabbing her coat and dashing from the room. "And I'm never coming back!"

"Fine!" Clarissa yelled, slamming her door.

She stood next to her door until she heard the front door slam. Then she climbed onto her bed and cried.

Chapter Twenty-eight

Mary opened the door and stepped aside so Bradley, carrying the garbage cans, could walk into the house unhindered.

"What's all this?" Margaret asked as Mary closed the door behind Bradley.

"Evidence," Bradley said, placing the garbage cans on the floor. "At least we hope so."

He looked around the room and then turned to Margaret. "Where are the girls?"

"Well, and there's a sad tale indeed," Margaret said kindly. "It seems that there was a disagreement upstairs, which caused Maggie to run home and Clarissa to stay up in her room, crying herself to sleep."

"Do you know what happened?" Mary asked. "They seemed fine when we left."

Margaret shook her head. "Ah, well, I do recall tempests in teapots when you were a little girl," she said. "I'm sure someone said something that made someone else feel sad. They will get over it." She paused and smiled. "Eventually."

"So, do we go over to the Brennans' tonight and talk to them about what happened?" Mary asked. "Or do we give them a couple of days to become friends again?"

"We've got to go over and meet with the Brennans tonight," Bradley said. "Whether we talk to them about the future is something we can decide, but we need to let them know what happened today."

Mary nodded. "You're right," she said. "But first we should put our evidence somewhere safe."

"Safe?" Margaret asked. "That doesn't sound good."

Mary slipped out of her coat and carried it to the closet. "Well, actually, we had a little company as we left the third floor," she explained. "But Bradley was able to come up with a brilliant escape plan."

"Escape?" Margaret exclaimed. "You had to escape?"

"Well, not exactly," Bradley inserted. "I don't think they were looking for us, but I think they knew someone was in that isolation unit today. We weren't in there long enough for anyone to see us and get over to the hospital."

Mary nodded. "That makes sense," she said. "And when we rushed past them on the gurney, they were focused on the unit, not us."

"Gurney?" Margaret asked. "Why did you need a gurney?"

Bradley grinned. "Because a man pushing a moaning, pregnant woman on a gurney tends to make potential bad guys overlook the two large garbage cans of evidence hidden beneath the sheets."

Margaret smiled. "That was a brilliant idea," she agreed. Then her smile disappeared. "But if they weren't looking for you, will they be looking for the girls?"

"It all depends on how they knew someone accessed the unit," Bradley said. "If there were sensors on the door, then all they would know is the door was opened."

"But if there were cameras," Mary said.

"Mike," Bradley called. "Mike, are you around?"

Mike appeared immediately. "Hey, what's up?" he asked.

"When you were at the hospital unit, did you notice any cameras?" Bradley asked.

"No, but I wasn't really looking," he admitted. "But give me a couple minutes and I can check it out."

"Thanks," Mary said. "That would be really helpful. Then we'll know what to say to the Brennans."

Mike turned back to Mary and Bradley. "You might want to have a chat with Clarissa about that," he said. "She might want to share a couple things with you."

"Okay," Bradley said. "We'll go right up."

Chapter Twenty-nine

Mary and Bradley walked down the street to the Brennans' home. The cold winter wind whipped around them, and Mary cuddled closer to Bradley. "Only a few more steps," Bradley said, hugging her. "And then we'll be there."

Mary smiled up at him. "It's just brisk, that's all."

They climbed up the stairs to the Brennan house, and Katie had the door opened before they knocked. "Hi! Come in quickly before you freeze," Katie said.

Following her in, they were instantly warmed by the crackling fire in the fireplace. A few minutes later, all four parents were gathered in overstuffed chairs around a coffee table in the living room with cups of hot tea in their hands.

"So, why the meeting?" Clifford asked.

"The girls had an incident this afternoon that we needed to talk to you about," Bradley said.

"Is everything okay?" Katie asked.

Mary nodded. "Well, yes and no," she said. "Clarissa overheard us talking about a case and decided that she and Maggie needed to help."

"What?" Clifford exclaimed. "What did they do?"

"They snuck away from my mother when they were visiting Stanley at the hospital, and took the elevator down to the third floor," Mary explained. "They ended up in a locked hallway and were frightened."

Katie met Mary's eyes. "Did they see anything…unusual?" she asked.

Mary nodded meaningfully. "Yes. Yes, they did," Mary replied. "And that was part of what frightened them."

"Were they harmed?" Clifford asked.

"No," Bradley said. "Both Margaret and I figured out where they were and arrived on the scene before they got too freaked out."

"Wait, the third floor," Clifford said. "Isn't that the floor that's having the rehab done on it?"

Mary nodded. "Yes. There are no patients, only empty rooms and some storage."

"So, anyone could have been hiding on that floor," Clifford replied. He turned to Mary. "Why wasn't your mother more aware of their presence."

"Well, the girls told her that they had to go to the bathroom," Mary explained. "And so, she thought they were only going a couple of doors down to the ladies' room."

"Maggie has mentioned Mike," Katie said to Mary. "Was he around?"

Mary smiled and nodded. "Yes, he was close by."

"Who is this Mike?" Clifford asked.

"A family friend," Bradley explained. "He was actually the first one to find the girls. He's a trained first responder."

"Did this have anything to do with those ghost stories Maggie keeps talking about?" Clifford asked.

"Yes, actually, it did," Mary said. "Would you like to hear the story behind it?"

Clifford shook his head. "No. That's not necessary," he said. "But I wish I knew how I could get Maggie to give that stuff up and just have a normal hobby."

Bradley coughed into his hand, hiding his smile. "I feel your pain," he finally was able to say. "But I have a feeling this is something that interests both of our daughters."

"So, do you think they should be punished for lying?" Clifford asked. "Are you going to ground Clarissa? Is that why she didn't come home with Maggie this afternoon?"

"I think the experience itself taught them a lesson," Bradley asked. "And they were actually trying to be helpful in the first place."

"And my mother mentioned that the girls had an argument," Mary added. "Maggie was pretty upset when she left, and Clarissa won't talk about it."

"Well, they'll come around," Katie said. "I'm sure of it."

"I hope so," Mary replied. "I really hope so."

Chapter Thirty

"Good morning, sweetheart," Mary said to Clarissa when she came down the stairs the next morning. "How did you sleep?"

Clarissa shrugged. "Fine, I guess,' she replied, slipping into a chair and resting her chin in her hands. "I don't think I'm feeling very good today."

"Well, let me check to see if you have a fever," Mary said, hiding her smile. She knew all too well why Clarissa didn't want to go to school, and there was no way she was going to get away with it. She leaned forward, placed her hand on Clarissa's forehead and waited there for a few moments. "No, you don't feel warm at all. No fever."

"I think my stomach hurts," Clarissa tried.

"Well, that's because you need breakfast," Bradley said as he came into the kitchen. "And since it's such a cold day outside, I think oatmeal might be just the thing."

Clarissa sighed. "Fine," she said. "I'll eat oatmeal."

Mary went back to the stove and scooped a bowl of oatmeal for Clarissa. She placed it in front of her at the table. "We went to the Brennans' last night," she said casually.

Clarissa perked up and turned to her. "Who did you see?" she asked.

"Just Katie and Clifford," Bradley said. "All the kids were already in bed."

"It's funny because when we came up to see you last night, you were already asleep too," Mary said. "I suppose you and Maggie were pretty tired from your adventure."

Clarissa shrugged and spooned brown sugar over her oatmeal.

"Are you going to walk over there and wait for the bus this morning?" Mary asked.

Clarissa shook her head and took a bite of the oatmeal. "No, I'm not," she said defiantly. "I'm not special enough to wait with Supergirl."

"Who is Supergirl?" Margaret asked, joining them in the kitchen.

"Oh, Maggie thinks she's extra special because she can see ghosts," Clarissa replied caustically.

"Well, that's a pretty cool thing," Bradley said.

Clarissa looked up at her father. "Well, you can't see ghosts, but you're still cool, right?" she asked.

"Yes, your father is very cool," Mary said. "And although seeing ghosts is a special gift, there are lots of special gifts in the world. Everyone having their own gift is what makes the world interesting."

"Well, some people think they're superheroes if they can see ghosts," Clarissa said, angrily biting down on the oatmeal. "They think they're specialer than anyone else."

Mary, Bradley and Margaret nodded at each other. The truth had finally come out.

"Well, I hope you can work it out," Bradley said. "You two have been friends for a long time."

Clarissa finished her food and then stood up. "Well, I guess maybe we've been friends for too long," she said. "I'm going to go brush my teeth, okay?"

"Okay, sweetheart," Mary said. "You have about ten minutes until the bus arrives."

They waited until they heard the bathroom door close.

"Hurt pride is tough," Bradley said softly.

"I think the only thing we can do is let them work it out," Mary said.

"That's one of the hardest things about parenting," Margaret said. "Not fixing it for them."

Chapter Thirty-one

Clarissa left the house just as the bus was pulling up so she could avoid speaking to Maggie. Mary watched from the window, and her heart ached for the two little girls who were trying so hard not to look at each other.

"Did they peek?" Margaret asked.

"Nope. Their faces were rock hard, and they just stared forward," Mary said. "It's going to be a long day for both of them."

"Might be longer than that," Margaret said.

"I can't believe they'll stay mad at each other for more than a couple of hours," Bradley said, slipping into his jacket. "My friends and I couldn't stay mad for more than a couple of minutes."

Mary and Margaret exchanged smiles. "Girls aren't the same as boys," Mary said. "Boys get mad, hit something and then it's done. Girls brood and get angrier as the day goes on. In a couple of hours, forgetting to say hi in a hallway turns into a national disaster."

Bradley shook his head. "No, you're teasing, right?"

Shaking her head, Mary sighed. "No, I'm afraid not," she replied. Then she smiled sweetly at him. "Oh, and it's going to get worse when she gets older."

"Wow, thanks for that," he replied. "I wonder if the Foreign Legion could use an extra soldier."

Laughing, Mary wagged her finger at him. "Oh no, we're in this together," she said. "For better or for worse, remember?"

He bent over and kissed her. "Good thing it's mostly for better," he said.

"Good thing," she replied. "Be safe out there."

He nodded. "You too."

Then he turned to Margaret. "Thank you for being here," he said. "I can't tell you how much your presence eases my mind."

She chuckled. "The pleasure is all mine," she said. "And it's so much more interesting at your house than at mine."

Bradley laughed. "Oh, yes, there is never a dull moment here. Have a great day."

Mary watched him leave, a smile on her face, and turned to see her mother watching her.

"You just glow when he's around," Margaret said. "And he's the same way. It makes me happy."

Mary sighed deeply. "He's the best thing that ever happened to me." Suddenly Mikey kicked her, and she jumped.

"What happened?" Margaret asked.

"Mikey just tried to kick me into the end zone," Mary replied.

"Well, perhaps he's jealous," Margaret teased.

Laughing, Mary rubbed her belly. "Okay, Mikey. You're also the best thing that ever happened to me." She looked up at her mom. "Two boys in the family. It's going to be interesting."

"Almost as interesting as two girls," her mother replied.

Nodding, Mary chuckled as she walked back into the kitchen with her mother. "So, what are you planning on doing today?" she asked.

Margaret put the bowls in the sink and turned on the hot water. "I was thinking about visiting with Stanley and Rosie at the hospital today," she said. "I really didn't get much of a chance to visit yesterday. Would that be all right with you?"

Mary nodded as she wiped down the table. "That would be great," she said. "I was going to go to the county building and see if I could discover anything about the children from the hospital."

Margaret studied her daughter as she leaned over the table, her belly getting in her way when she tried to reach the other side. "Do you think you should try and take it easy? Relax and put your feet up?"

Mary laughed. "I think that would drive me crazy," she replied. "Besides, Mikey's not supposed to come until the end of the month, so I have plenty of time to take it easy before then."

"First babies can come early," Margaret warned.

Mary shook her head. "No, I'm not going to even consider that," she said. "Or I'll go crazy during my last week of pregnancy. And, speaking of pregnancy, Bradley and I have a birthing class we're supposed to attend on Friday night. Would you mind staying with Clarissa?"

"A Friday night girl's night?" Margaret said with a smile. "Oh, I think we can manage to have a good time together."

Mary came over and hugged her mom. "Thanks, Ma," she said. "You are the greatest."

Chapter Thirty-two

Bradley opened the fourth manila folder and typed the name of the child onto his computer screen. The system didn't have any information about that individual, but when he entered the name of the guardian, he got an immediate hit. Her list of priors went down three screen lengths and mostly included solicitation, drunken and disorderly, and passing bad checks.

"Real winner for a mom," Bradley muttered as he reviewed the list. And when he got to final entry he swore softly. Another dead parent and the child remanded to the custody of the state.

Bradley flipped the file across his desk and stood up, ran his hand through his hair as he exhaled sharply and walked over to the door of his office. "Dorothy," he said, as he approached his assistant's desk. "I need to speak with the CEO of the hospital." He nodded slowly as he thought about it. "Yeah, I need to speak with him right away."

She picked up the phone and held it in her hand for a moment. "Do you want me to set up something in his office at the hospital or do you want me to send a couple of uniforms to pick him up?" she asked with a slight smile.

Bradley smiled back. "Offer him the choice," he said with a shrug. "And let him know I'm on my way there."

"Yes, sir," Dorothy said.

"Thank you," he said, turning to walk down the hall.

"Oh, and boss," Dorothy called, her ear to the phone.

He turned back, expectantly.

"I love it when you kick butt and take names," she replied.

He smiled and nodded. "Sometimes that's what you've got to do."

Hurrying down the stairs, he pulled his phone from his pocket and punched in Mary's number.

"Hi handsome." Her answer immediately put a smile on his face.

"Hey, gorgeous," he replied. "I'm taking a field trip."

"Really? How exciting for you," she replied. "And where are you going?"

"I decided to meet with the CEO of the hospital," he said. "I want to find out what he knows."

"Great idea," Mary replied. "Follow the money."

"Yeah. Exactly," he replied. "How are you feeling?"

"I'm good," she replied. "I've got an appointment with Linda at the Courthouse in about fifteen minutes, I want to see if she has any records that will shed more light on this."

"Well, bundle up," he said. "It's cold and windy out here."

"I will," she said. "Hey, Ma's at the hospital, visiting Stanley and Rosie. So, if you get done giving him the third degree and still have some time, you should go up and say hi."

"If they don't kick me out of the hospital," he said.

"They can't kick you out of the hospital," she said. "We have a birthing class on Friday night and you have to go with me."

Bradley clicked open the lock of his cruiser and climbed in. "Or, we could do something else," he said. "Like...I don't know...anything."

"Bradley, it will be fun," she said.

He put the key into the ignition and turned his car on, switching his phone to the cruiser's Bluetooth speaker. "I don't think it will be fun," he replied, putting the car in reverse and pulling out his parking spot. "I don't think it will even remotely resemble fun."

"That's because you don't know what fun really is," Mary teased.

Bradley put the car in forward and pulled into the street. "Hmmm, let me see," he continued. "Sitting in a class, watching movies of women giving birth in full color, that just doesn't sound like fun to me."

"Bradley," Mary said, letting her dramatic sigh travel through the phone line.

"But for you," he said. "I would do anything. Even go to a birthing class."

"Thank you," she replied. "We can go out for ice cream afterwards."

"Can we drive to the park and neck?" he asked.

"It'll be dark," she said. "We might get arrested."

"I think I can take care of that," he assured her. "Hey, I'm at the hospital. I love you."

"I love you too," she replied. "Have fun."

"Oh, yeah, I will," he assured her. "Be safe."

Chapter Thirty-three

Bradley was right, Mary thought as she walked from her office to the County Courthouse. It was really cold and windy outside. She hurried down the street, pulled open the door to the building and slipped inside. The security guard smiled at her. "Pretty cold out there," he said.

She nodded. "Yeah, very cold," she agreed.

She put her purse on the counter and walked through the metal detector. The guard glanced through her purse and then handed it to her.

"So, you still pregnant?" he teased, laughing at his own joke.

Mary smiled weakly. "Yes. Yes, I am," she replied. "I'm not due until the end of the month."

"Are you kidding me?" he exclaimed. "You're as big as a house."

Mary paused and stared at him. Really? Did he think she needed to hear that?

"Okay, well, I'll see you later," she finally said and turned without giving him a chance to respond.

"As big as a house," she muttered as she walked down the hallway to Linda's office. "You still pregnant?"

"Mary, you're talking to yourself," Linda said, coming up alongside her.

Mary smiled at her friend, the newly appointed county administrator. "How's the new job?" she asked.

"Great. Busy. Crazy," Linda replied. "But I really love it."

She led Mary into her office and offered her a chair. "So," Linda asked as she sat down, "what can I do for you?"

"I've got a client, actually several clients, who were in an isolation ward at Freeport Hospital," she explained. "It was in the mid-nineties, and I think they might have been given some experimental drugs for AIDS."

"Are they thinking about taking legal action against the hospital?" she asked.

Mary shook her head. "No, Linda, they all died," she said.

"Oh, I'm so sorry," Linda replied. "Would there have been any kind of consent forms filled out?"

Mary shook her head. "They were all under the age of eight," she said.

"Under the age of eight?" Linda exclaimed. "And you think they were given experimental drug treatments?"

"That's what it looks like," Mary said. "There were thirteen patients, and once they had all passed away, they closed the study or whatever it was they were doing."

"Did the parents or guardians give consent?" Linda asked.

"Bradley's still looking into that," she said. "But so far, most of the children were guardians of the State."

Linda stood up. "Come on, Mary," she said. "Let's take a walk. There are some files I'd like to look through."

Mary nodded. "I was really hoping you'd say that."

They left Linda's office and walked down the hall to the staircase, taking it down to the basement of the building. At the end of the hall was a large vault door that stood slightly ajar. "We converted most of the old records to an electronic format," Linda explained. "But some of the files from the nineties didn't get converted, so I thought we could check here first."

They slipped into the large, metal-lined room. Aisles of shelves ran from the back of the room to the front and stood about four feet apart. On the shelves were white cardboard boxes with fitted lids. On the outside of the boxes was a description of the files they held and the date they were stored in the vault.

"Okay, we should look for DCFS files from the nineties," Linda said. "And I think they might be back here in this aisle."

They walked down the aisle that towered above them. Mary looked up at the top shelves about twelve feet up. "Let's hope the files aren't all the way up there," Mary said.

Linda looked up. "Yeah, I agree," she said. "Because there's no way you're going to be climbing a ladder in your condition, which means I would have to do it."

Mary laughed. "Well, I'm suddenly feeling a lot less worried about files in those high shelves," she said. "But, don't worry, I'll be down here on the floor cheering you on."

"Thanks," Linda replied. "Thanks a lot."

She stopped in front of a section nearest to the back wall. "This should be where they are," Linda said.

"Unless someone moved them to the top shelf," Mary suggested.

"Funny," Linda replied as she squatted down in front of the lowest shelf. "Let's see." She looked at the dates in front of her. "This one is from August of 1997. What do you think?"

"Actually, that sounds like a good date," Mary replied. "I remember that one of the journal entries was from that date."

Linda pulled the box from the shelf and lifted the top. "Do you have any names?" she asked.

"Well, one of the children is Jack Dunne," Mary said. "He was six when he died."

Linda flipped slowly through the files, and finally she shook her head. "No. No Jack Dunne in here," she said. "Any other names?"

"Anna Nevin," Mary volunteered. "She was eight when she died. She's the oldest in the group."

Linda went through each file in the box and shook her head again. "Sorry, none of the files have either of those names," she said. "Although…"

"Although what?" Mary asked.

Linda pulled out a thick file. "Although this one is odd," she said. "It doesn't have a name associated with it. All it says is Baker's Dozen."

"That's them," Mary exclaimed. "There were thirteen of them, and they were referred to as a baker's dozen."

Linda put the top back on the box and pushed it back onto the shelf. Then she handed Mary the file. "Just remember," she said. "You didn't get that from me."

Mary smiled. "Do I even know you?" she asked.

Linda laughed and nodded. "Exactly."

Chapter Thirty-four

"Knock, knock," Margaret called from the outside of Stanley's room. "It's Margaret O'Reilly."

"Come in," Rosie called. "We're all decent."

"Speak fer yourself," Stanley said.

Margaret chuckled as she stood behind the curtain that was drawn across the doorway. "Well, I don't know if I should come in or leave," Margaret said.

Stanley laughed. "Take a chance," he called. "Come on in."

She walked around the curtain. "Okay, I'm taking a chance."

Rosie rushed to greet Margaret with a hug. "It's so good to see you again," Rosie said. "How are you enjoying your visit?"

"Well, there's never a dull moment in that household," Margaret said.

"That's fer sure," Stanley agreed. "I'm hoping that Mary listened to my advice and didn't try nothing funny with that little girl ghost down on the third floor. She's got enough to worry about with the baby and all."

Margaret followed Rosie over to Stanley's bedside, and they both sat down. "Well, as a matter of fact," Margaret said, "there are actually thirteen ghost children on the third floor. And, not only did Mary get involved, but so did Clarissa and Maggie."

"Thirteen children?" Rosie exclaimed. "How could there be thirteen ghost children in the hospital?"

"I'm guessing they died," Stanley grumbled. "That's how most ghosts are made."

Rosie turned to Stanley, her lips tight. "Stanley, you know exactly what I meant," she scolded lightly. "Why are there so many ghosts down there?"

"Well, I'm not saying I know anything about those kids," Stanley replied. "But I can tell you there's quite a few stories about ghosts in this here hospital."

"Really?" Margaret asked.

Stanley nodded. "From what these nurses tell me, there are ghosts on every floor," he said, lowering his voice slightly. "They've even seen some near this very room."

Rosie shivered and looked around. "Do you think there are ghosts in here, with us, now?" she asked.

"Could be," Stanley said, holding back a smile. "You just never know when a ghost will appear out of nowhere."

Rosie wrapped her arms around herself. "Now, you're just trying to scare me," she said.

Stanley chuckled. "And I'm doing a purty good job of it, if I do say so myself."

Margaret shook her head. "Now that's just mean, Stanley," she said with a good-natured smile. "Stop scaring Rosie, or she might just leave you to entertain yourself."

Rosie smiled at Margaret and then turned to Stanley. "She's absolutely right," she said pointedly. "I have a lot to do at home to get things organized for when you're released from the hospital."

"Where is home?" Margaret asked. "I thought your house caught fire."

"Stanley's house caught fire," Rosie said. "We'd been renting my house to a young family, but luckily, our tenants had moved a month before Christmas and we hadn't rented it again."

"Well that was fortunate," Margaret said.

"Yes, it really was," Rosie agreed. "And the damage to Stanley's house was mostly in the living room, so I was able to salvage things that didn't smell like smoke."

"So, when are you getting released?" Margaret asked Stanley.

"Not soon enough," Stanley grumbled. "But they're talking about a week or so more. Seems like my burns are healing up pretty well."

"Well then, you should be out of the hospital before Mary goes in," Margaret replied with a smile.

Stanley's face softened. "Sure seems like that baby's taken forever to get here."

"If it feels that way to us," Rosie added, "just think about how Mary's been feeling."

"I'm sure she is more than ready to have her baby," Margaret said. "More than ready!"

Chapter Thirty-five

"I am so not ready to have this baby," Mary
told Mike as they sat together in her office. "I have so
much to do still."

"The other things will get done," he said.
"Mikey and your well-being need to be your first
priority."

She studied him for a moment. He hadn't
really made eye contact during the last five minutes
he'd been in her office. "What are you not telling
me?" she asked.

"Mary, if I'm not telling you something," he
said, "it's because I'm not supposed to be telling you
something."

She shook her head. "Nope, I'm not going to
take that for an answer," she said. "I don't want to
know when Mikey's going to be born. I get that's
need-to-know information, but there's something else
going on. What is it?"

He floated away from her and slowly floated around her office. "When does the lease expire for this office, Mary?" he asked.

Shaking her head, Mary stared at him. "Okay, that was a random question," she said. "But, to answer your question, it ends February 1st. Why?"

He turned and met her eyes. "I would suggest that you not renew your lease."

"Not renew…" she stopped and stared at him. Thoughts and ideas, fears mostly, rushed through her mind.

"Am I going to die?" she stammered.

"No!" he replied with a frustrated sigh. "No. Of course not. No."

"Well, thank goodness," she replied, exhaling loudly. "Okay, you are really freaking me out, and I don't need to be freaked out right now. Can't you just tell me what's going on?"

Mike looked around slowly and then quickly floated back to her desk. "I can tell you a few things to ease your mind," he said. "First, you need to remember to have faith. Even when things look like you can't handle it, or life is totally messed up, you need to have faith."

"Can I just say, that did not ease my mind," Mary replied.

He smiled. "God loves you, Mary," he said softly. "Remember that. He loves you."

She nodded. "I can remember that," she said.

"Not just remember," Mike said emphatically. "Believe it. Believe that He loves you."

"Okay," she said hesitantly. "I believe it. What else?"

He paused, and Mary could tell he was thinking about how to say something.

"Just say it," Mary prompted. "You don't need to pull any punches with me."

He smiled at her. "That's true," he replied. "If anyone can handle anything, it's you."

"What do I have to handle?" she asked, concerned.

He grinned. "You are so suspicious," he teased.

"Mike, what do I need to handle?" she demanded.

"Change," he said. "You're going to need to handle change."

She continued to meet his eyes. "Okay," she replied. "I'm going to have a baby. That's a huge change for me and, really, for our whole family. But I think I'm ready for it. Well, as ready as I'm going to be."

"I thought you just said that you weren't ready to have this baby," Mike reminded her.

"I meant that in a 'I have so much to do before the baby is born' kind of way," she amended. "Not, I'm not ready — ready."

His grin spread wider. "Oh, well, that makes total sense," he said.

"I'm ready," she said. "But I know having a baby will change my life."

He nodded, and the smile left his face. "Yes, it will," he said meaningfully.

"See, it's comments like that that give me heartburn," she said.

He chuckled softly and leaned forward to press a chaste kiss on her forehead. "God isn't the only one who loves you, Mary," he said, and then he disappeared.

"That's not fair," she yelled into the empty room. "That's not fair at all."

Chapter Thirty-six

Bradley walked through the hospital lobby with a purposeful stride. He meant business, and he wanted to be sure that anyone reporting to the CEO could see that. He walked past the emergency room seating, down the hall past the lab section, and towards the administrative offices.

"Hey, Chief!"

Bradley stopped and turned to see the maintenance man he'd stopped yesterday for a key jogging to catch him.

"Hi," Bradley said, maintaining his serious attitude. "What's up?"

The maintenance man looked around, checking to see if anyone else was within ear shot, and even when he determined no one was, he still lowered his voice. "I just wanted to let you know that I heard they were going to up the demolition of the third floor," he whispered.

"What?" Bradley asked.

The man nodded. "Yeah, I thought you might want to know," he said. "Some guys showed up yesterday, late afternoon, and told the CEO they wanted it done by the end of next week. But, you know, it takes time to get the equipment, so the CEO told them we'd start next Friday."

Next Friday. That's how long we have to figure this out and get those kids to crossover, Bradley thought.

"Thank you," Bradley said. "This is important to know. I really appreciate it."

The man shrugged. "Hey, you probably don't remember," he said. "But I'm Mel Marcum. We met about a year ago. You helped save my son. He was kidnapped."

This time Bradley did smile. "I do remember," he said. "How's your family?"

"My wife is great," he said. "She...well, you know...she still is grieving for Joey. But it's getting better. It's like Joey's our guardian angel or something. It's like we can feel his presence."

Bradley nodded. "I know exactly what you mean," he replied.

Mel shook his head. "And we still get an occasional whiff of dog," he said, perplexed.

Bradley thought about the ghost dog that had followed Mary and had finally been adopted by Joey. "Well, you know, Joey always wanted a dog," Bradley said without thinking.

Mel looked even more confused. "Yeah, he did," he said. "But how did you know that?"

Bradley shrugged. "You must have mentioned it," he replied. "How else could I know?"

Mel nodded slowly. "Yeah, right," he said. "How else?"

Bradley pulled out his card and handed it to Mel. "If you hear anything else you think I should know, please give me a call," he said. "And, if your family ever needs anything, please keep in touch."

Mel shoved the card in his pocket. "I will, thanks," he said. "Great to see you."

"You too," Bradley replied. "Take care."

Bradley continued his walk to the administrative offices and entered the executive wing. The CEO's assistant immediately stood up when she saw him and hurried forward. "We received the call from your office," she said. "And, of course, Dr. Claeys is happy to make time to see you."

Bradley nodded. "That was a good decision," he said briskly.

The assistant gasped softly and nodded. "Please, go straight in," she said. "He's waiting for you."

"Thank you," Bradley replied.

The office was quite luxurious, with a large, highly polished, wooden desk, and leather chairs both around the desk and in a separate sitting area with a gas fireplace. The walls and shelves were lined with fine art and sculptures. Bradley gave a cursory glance around the room and walked to the desk where Dr. Claeys sat, nervously tapping his pen against his leather blotter.

"Claeys," Bradley said with a nod, taking a seat in a chair in front of the desk. "I have a few questions for you."

Claeys nodded, and Bradley noted the drops of perspiration dotting his upper lip.

"Before I ask you any questions," Bradley continued, "and read you your rights in this ongoing investigation, I thought I would give you the opportunity to tell me what you know. So I can tell the judge in the case that you came to me, freely, in order to help me close this case."

"This all happened before I was here," Claeys blurted nervously. "I had nothing to do with the contract."

Bradley didn't say a word, only studied Claeys silently.

"Okay. Okay," the doctor blurted out. "I did know that we were receiving monthly payments from them for the rent of the space on the third floor."

Bradley sat back slowly and folded his arms across his chest.

"Fine," the doctor stammered. "I was told about the drug trials. But I didn't make any of those decisions. I didn't administer the drugs to the kids. I wasn't even on the staff at the time."

"Who?" Bradley asked and smiled to himself as he wondered what kind of valuable information the doctor would blurt out.

"Dr. Reinsband," Claeys said. "Reinsband had the medical contract with the pharmaceutical company. We just had the facility contract. Reinsband injected all the children, monitored the effects and created the study. All we did was house the study."

Bradley lifted an eyebrow in disbelief.

"Okay, fine," Claeys said. "We worked with DCFS to get the participants."

"Victims," Bradley inserted.

"Listen, they all had AIDS," he said. "None of them had any way to pay for treatment. These drugs could have worked. These drugs could have saved their lives…"

Claeys stammered to a halt when Bradley glared at him. "These drugs had side effects," he said slowly. "Painful, debilitating side effects. You were not trying to cure these children. You were using them as guinea pigs."

He pulled out his phone, pressed a number and waited until the call was answered.

"Alex," Bradley said, speaking to Alex Boettcher, the Stephenson County District Attorney. "I'm sitting in the office of Dr. Claeys at the hospital. I have a strong feeling that he wants to make an official statement about a drug trial held here in the hospital in which minors were used." He waited and nodded. "Yes, I can wait for you to arrive. Thanks."

He hung up his phone and looked at Dr. Claeys.

"Should I call my lawyer?" Dr. Claeys asked, his face ashen.

Bradley shrugged. "Well, if I were Alex and I learned from the police chief that the CEO of the hospital had contacted the police when he discovered some shady dealings at the hospital, I would wonder why his lawyer was also in the room."

"You would say that?" Claeys asked. "You would say that I called you?"

"I haven't been questioning you, have I?" Bradley asked. "You have offered me all of this information freely. I have no problem telling Alex that you have been cooperating with the police department from the start."

Claeys sighed with relief. "Okay. Good. Great," he said. "I'll make a statement."

Bradley nodded, and then he leaned forward in his chair while Claeys tried to shrink back into his. "But if I find out that you have withheld information from me or Alex," Bradley threatened, "all bets are off."

Claeys swallowed loudly and then nodded. "Yes. Of course. Fine," he stammered. "I will cooperate to the fullest extent."

"Where's Reinsband?" Bradley asked.

"He retired several years ago," Claeys said. "He's in a nursing home now."

"Thank you," Bradley replied. "And do you have any information about the DCFS agent who handled these kids?"

Claeys shook his head briskly. "No. No. I don't know about that."

"Okay," Bradley said, slowly leaning back in his chair. "Is there anyone else who worked the unit who is still connected with the hospital?"

"There is one nurse…" Claeys said hesitantly.

"I think it would be a good idea to have the nurse join us," he said. "Now."

Chapter Thirty-seven

Mary flipped through the sheets of paper inside the file Linda had given her. All of the children had been alone— no parents, no relatives, no guardians of any kind. The State was supposed to have been their safety net, but the State ended up being their worst nightmare.

One name kept reappearing on the forms as the DCFS caseworker responsible for all of the children who were part of the Baker's Dozen— Carol Ford.

Mary put the name in her search engine and didn't come up with anything local at all. "That's odd," she whispered. "She doesn't even have a Facebook page."

She picked up her phone and dialed Linda. "Hi," she said when Linda answered. "This is someone you don't know."

Linda laughed. "Well, good," she finally replied. "What do you need?"

"The caseworker for all of these kids was Carol Ford," she said. "I can't find anything about her."

"Carol Ford," Linda repeated slowly. "Why do I know that name?"

"Well, it's a good sign that you know her name," Mary said. "Anything coming to you?"

Linda sighed. "No, it's not," she said. "But there's something there." She paused. "Why don't you let me think about it, and I'll call you back later today."

"That would be great," she said. "And in the meantime, I'll head over to the Freeport Republic and chat with my favorite editor."

"Oh, good idea," Linda said. "Jerry is like a walking database on Freeport news. He'll probably know immediately."

"If he remembers, I'll call you so you can stop thinking," Mary said.

"Thanks," Linda laughed. "Then I can use my brain power on something else."

Mary was still smiling when she walked to her car. It was nice to have a friend like Linda who didn't take herself too seriously. The drive to the Freeport Republic took less time than finding a parking spot. Finally, Mary pulled in behind the paper's building next to the loading dock. Dutch, the forty-year veteran of the circulation crew, was standing on the dock next to the door. He waved at her when she approached.

"No jokes about getting a fork-lift to help me up," Mary said. "Okay?"

"Are you kidding?" he replied. "You look gorgeous. But I am going to help you up those steps. They might be slick."

He hurried down and with Mary's arm wrapped within his, carefully guided her up the steps to the dock level. "You know, you're not supposed to look this good when you're pregnant," he said. "How come that husband of yours is letting you out alone?"

"Dutch, you know you were always my first choice," she teased.

"Yeah, don't let my wife hear that," he said.

"She wouldn't mind," Mary said. "Because you always chose her."

"So, what's up?" he asked as he led her inside where it was warm.

"I need to speak with Jerry," she said.

"Are you sure you want to go in there?" he asked. "He's in a mood."

"Is he ever not in a mood?" she teased.

"You got me there," he replied. "Okay, you know your way there. Good luck, kid."

She was surprised that the smell of ink and mechanical oil didn't turn her stomach. The chemical smell was pungent and metallic, but oddly appealing. The large presses weren't running, so the room was quiet as she maneuvered around the massive machines inhabiting the press room to get to the door to the newsroom.

Pushing open the door, she looked around at the bustling energy of the reporters hurrying to meet the daily deadline. Row upon row of ancient metal desks with high tech computers lit up the room. The sound of fingers on keyboards echoed throughout the room as the staff focused on their work.

"Hey, Mary, how are you doing?"

Mary looked over to see her friend Jane, the head photographer for the paper, waving her over. She walked down the narrow aisle to Jane's workspace. "Hey, what's up?" Mary asked.

"I wanted to show you something interesting," Jane said, clicking her mouse on a file folder. "I was here at the paper late one night, testing some photography equipment when I took some photos of the newsroom."

She clicked on a final thumbnail, and a large image appeared on the screen. "Look," she said. "Do you see that, in the corner?"

Mary peered at the photo and saw a blurry image in the corner. "What is that?" she asked Jane.

"I don't know," Jane replied. "It wasn't in the other photos I took of the same area a few minutes later."

Mary lifted her head and looked over to the spot Jane had photographed. The ghost of Anna

Paxton, a former society columnist for the paper, grinned at her. The paper had been Anna's life and now, it seemed, was also her death.

"I think it's Anna," Jane breathed, still looking at the blurry image on the screen. "I actually thought I could smell cigarette smoke."

Anna had been notorious for her several pack a day cigarette addiction.

"Well, she loved working here," Mary replied. "And she certainly had a fondness for you. If she would appear to anyone, she would appear to you."

"So, do you think I've got something here?" Jane asked, her voice edged with excitement.

"In my humble opinion, I really think that you do."

"Hey, O'Reilly, are you paying my staff for entertaining you?" Jerry Wiley, the editor-in-chief, called from across the room.

Jane rolled her eyes. "Okay, back to work," she grumbled. "Thanks for looking."

"Thanks for sharing," Mary said, and then she walked across the room toward Jerry.

"Just the man I was looking for," she said.

"Funny, Jane and I don't look at all alike," he replied sarcastically. "And yet, there you were wasting her time while we're on deadline."

Mary shrugged. "She was showing me a picture she captured the other night of a glowing entity standing near your office door," she said casually.

"What?" Jerry exclaimed.

"Yeah, she thinks it was Anna," Mary continued, biting back a smile. Jerry had encountered Anna's ghost several times, although he would never admit it. "She actually thought she smelled cigarette smoke."

"Do you think it was Anna?" Jerry asked, his voice lowered.

Mary looked past Jerry, through the glass walls, to the inside of his office, and then she shrugged. "Could have been," she said. "Although, Anna prefers to be inside your office."

Jerry's face turned pale, and he slowly looked over his shoulder. "Inside?" he asked.

With a wide grin on her face, Anna swiped across Jerry's desk, sending a pile of papers cascading down from the desktop. But all Jerry could see were the papers suddenly moving by themselves.

Mary turned to Jerry. "That's odd," she said evenly. "I didn't feel a breeze."

"There wasn't one," Jerry muttered. He paused at the entrance of his office for a long moment and then cautiously went inside. He pointed to a Naugahyde and metal chair in front of his desk. "Take a load off, O'Reilly."

She sat down and smiled at Anna. Anna winked at her before she glided out of the room.

Jerry looked out the glass walls and, once satisfied that no one was watching, leaned forward across his desk. "Is Anna in here?" he whispered. "You can tell me."

Mary shook her head. "I can honestly tell you that Anna is not in this room with us," she said. "And now I have a question for you. Who is Carol Ford?"

"Carol Ford?" Jerry repeated. "What the hell do you want know about her for? Did she escape or something?"

"Escape?" Mary asked.

"Yeah, she was convicted of embezzling government funds," he said. "Her bank account had tens of thousands of dollars in it. You don't make that kind of money as a caseworker."

Mary studied Jerry. He wasn't telling her everything.

"What?" she asked.

He grinned. "You don't get put away for thirty years for embezzling," he said. "No one gets put away for that long…unless."

"Unless what?" Mary asked.

"Unless someone wanted her put away and shut up," he said. "Someone powerful."

"What prison did she go to?" Mary asked.

Jerry's smile widened. "Well, you are one lucky lady," he said. "She's at the Stephenson County Jail."

Chapter Thirty-eight

Bradley stood up when the older woman entered Dr. Claeys' office, and the woman paused at the doorway, fear apparent in her eyes.

"Maya, thank you for coming down," the doctor said. "This is Police Chief Alden."

She nodded and had to clear her throat twice before she could speak. "Chief," she finally mumbled.

"Ms. Alvarez," Bradley said. "I'd like to ask you a couple of questions."

She nodded and bit her lower lip. "Okay," she replied.

"District Attorney Alex Boettcher is on his way here," Bradley said. "I'd really like him to be here before I ask you any questions."

She looked nervously from Bradley to Claeys. "I, um, I'm only on my break," she said. "The others will be expecting me back."

Claeys pressed a button on his phone.

"Beverly, call up to Maya's area and let them know that I'm keeping Maya here for a little while. Help them find someone who can take over her shift for a while."

He released the button and looked up at the nurse. "You don't have to worry about getting back now," he said. He glanced toward Bradley and then back to Maya. "And I would really like you to cooperate with this investigation."

Maya shook her head. "I don't know anything about anything," she said.

Bradley nodded. "Well, I guess we'll confirm that once the DA gets here."

"I think I want a lawyer here," she said. "I don't have to talk to you."

Bradley nodded. "You're right," he said. "You don't have to say a word. But I want you to know that at this point, I'm just asking questions and trying to understand what went on in that unit. You need to decide if you want your version of the story told upfront or later on, once other people tell their account."

She shook her head. "I don't know," she said. "I don't know what I should do."

"Well, why don't you listen for a while," Alex said as he walked into the office. "And then you can decide."

Alex turned to Bradley and held out his hand. "Alden," he said, shaking his hand and smiling with affection. "Good to see you. How's Mary?"

"As gorgeous as ever," Bradley said. "The baby's due at the end of the month."

"You are one lucky son-of-a-gun," Alex replied. Then Alex turned to Claeys and Maya. "I'm District Attorney Alex Boettcher," he said. "And you are?"

"I'm Maya Alvarez," she said. "I'm a nurse at the hospital."

"Good to meet you, Ms. Alvarez," he said.

Dr. Claeys stood up and walked over to Alex. "I'm Doctor Charles Claeys," he said. "I'm the CEO of the hospital."

Alex nodded, his face losing the friendly expression it held when he was conversing with

Bradley. "Let's get started," he said. He put his leather briefcase on the coffee table near the leather chairs and opened it up. He first pulled out a small digital recorder and set it on the table. Then he pulled out a legal pad and pen.

"Why doesn't everyone take a seat over here," he suggested. "That way the recorder can pick up your voice." He turned to his friend. "Chief Alden, why don't you give me a quick overview of the situation."

Bradley nodded. "I have, in my possession, a collection of files dating back to the 1990s," he said. "There are thirteen of them. Each file records the medical responses juvenile patients were having to experimental drugs being used on them to treat AIDS."

"How did you discover these records?" Alex asked.

"Mary was following up on an investigation," Bradley said, meeting Alex's eyes.

"Ahhh, well, I should have known," he said. "And these children?"

"All died of AIDS-related complications," Bradley replied.

"Did their parents consent to the application of these trial drugs?" Alex asked.

"All of the children were wards of the State under the protection of DCFS," Bradley explained. "It seems that the State relinquished their rights and their well-being to a Dr. Reinsband and, I'm assuming, a pharmaceutical company."

Alex put his pen down and met Bradley's eyes. "How bad was it?" he asked softly.

"From what I've read, it was agony for these children," he replied, his voice tense with anger. "These children suffered side effects like swollen joints, cramps, diarrhea and nausea. If they refused to take the medicine, they were force fed the pills and given injections. It was basically a torture chamber."

Maya bent her head towards her lap and started to sob.

"Ms. Alvarez," Alex said, his voice cool. "Do you have something to add?"

She lifted her head, her eyes red and swollen. "I didn't know," she said. "I didn't know the drugs were causing those effects. They told me it was the AIDS. I swear, they told me it was the AIDS."

Chapter Thirty-nine

"Linda," Mary said through the Bluetooth connection in her car. "Jerry remembered her. She was convicted of embezzlment and sent to Stephenson County Jail."

"It's so much easier to remember when people tell you what happened," Linda replied. "So, what are you going to do?"

"I'm going to try and visit her," Mary said. "From what Jerry said, it sounds like her sentence may have been longer in order to silence her. I'd like to hear what she has to say."

"Okay, but be careful," Linda said. "If what Jerry says is true, there may still be some people in high places who don't want this truth to be exposed."

"Well, I'm not going to try and go today," she said. "Mikey and I have a doctor's appointment."

"Well, good luck with that," Linda replied. "And let me know if I can help you in any way."

"Thanks, Linda," Mary replied. "I appreciate it."

Mary drove to her doctor's office near the college and parked. A gust of wind just about knocked her back inside the car, but she pushed against it and made it to the office building.

"Mary, how are you feeling?" the receptionist asked her.

"I'm great," Mary replied. "And Mikey's learned to do River Dance. He especially enjoys it late at night, when I'm trying to sleep."

The receptionist nodded sympathetically. "The last few weeks of pregnancy are the worst," she said. "But pretty soon you'll have that cute baby in your arms, and it will all have been worth it."

Mary shook her head slowly. "You know, it's funny. I do realize, logically, that pregnancy only lasts nine months and eventually I'll have a baby to show for it," she said. "But there's this illogical part of me that feels like I'm just going to be pregnant forever. I can't even imagine holding Mikey yet."

"Maybe you feel that way because the amount of love you will feel for Mikey once he's here is unimaginable," the receptionist suggested. "It's immediate and powerful. It's like suddenly you are a momma bear, ready to protect your baby from anything."

Mary rested her hands on her belly. "I kind of feel that way already," she said.

The receptionist shook her head. "Oh, you've haven't felt anything like it yet."

"Wow," Mary said. "I can't wait."

Walking to the waiting area, Mary pulled out her phone to check her messages. There was a text from Clarissa's teacher letting her know that there seemed to be a problem between Clarissa and Maggie.

Mary texted back. *Thanks for letting me know. I was hoping they would make up today. Were there any problems at school?*

The teacher texted back immediately. *No. No problem. It's just weird to see those two apart. But I'm sure they'll get over it.*

"I hope so," Mary muttered.

Just then she was called back to the examination room. She pushed herself out of the chair and walked toward the nurse.

"How are you feeling?" the nurse asked.

"Good," Mary replied. "For the most part."

"The most part?" the nurse asked as they walked back to the room.

"I have found that my temper is not quite as even as it used to be," Mary confessed. "Especially with people who feel they need to comment on your pregnancy."

The nurse chuckled softly. "Things like, hey, isn't that baby here yet?" she asked.

"Exactly," Mary replied. "Or, are you still pregnant? I want to turn to them and say, 'No, I had the baby three months ago. This is just holiday overeating.'"

"I would love to see the expression on their face if you answered like that," the nurse laughed. "We once had a woman break someone's nose when he asked a question."

Mary stopped mid-stride. "Are you kidding?" she asked.

The nurse shook her head. "No, she was about a week overdue. Her back was killing her. Her feet

216

were swollen. And she had been working all day," the nurse explained. "A co-worker came over to her and said something like 'You haven't had that baby yet?'"

"Oh no," Mary said.

The nurse shrugged. "I don't think she even thought about it," she said. "She just whipped her fist around and nailed the guy. Luckily he didn't press charges."

"Why didn't he?" Mary asked.

"I heard that when his wife heard what happened she told him that he was lucky to still be alive."

Mary laughed aloud. "Be afraid of tired, pregnant women," she said. "Be very afraid."

Chapter Forty

The sight of Alex and Bradley walking side by side down the hallway of the hospital turned more than one female head. They matched each other stride for stride, their gazes intent, their faces somber.

"Where can we talk?" Alex asked.

"Mary's office," Bradley replied. "I'll let her know we're coming."

Alex nodded. "Good. Great," he said. "I need to decide what the next steps are."

"Yeah" Bradley said. They walked out of the hospital into the parking lot. Bradley looked around, making sure they were alone. "I learned from a friend that they've moved up the demolition schedule. The unit is supposed to be torn down in about ten days."

"Ten days?" Alex said.

"Yeah, Friday the thirteenth," Bradley replied.

Alex inhaled sharply. "Mary's office," he said.

"In five minutes," Bradley agreed.

They both separated to go to their vehicles in different areas of the parking lot. Bradley pulled out his cell and called Mary. "Hey, are you at your office?" he asked as soon as she answered her phone.

"Yes," she replied. "I just got back from my doctor's appointment. But I'm here."

"How did it go?" he asked.

"I got a clean bill of health until next week," she replied. "Mikey and I are both doing great."

"That's great news," he said. "Alex and I are on the way over. We need to compare notes."

"Excellent," she said. "Because I've got some interesting information to add to your notes."

He smiled. "I thought you might," he said. "Okay, I'm at my car. See you in about five minutes."

He hung up with Mary, unlocked the cruiser and climbed in. As soon as he started the car, he received a call from Dorothy at the office.

"Alden," he answered.

"This isn't Dorothy, and I'm not calling you from the privacy of your office so the mayor can't see me," Dorothy said. "Just so we're both clear about that."

Bradley experienced a sinking feeling in the pit of his stomach. "Okay," he said hesitantly. "Why are you not calling me?"

"I'm not telling you that a group of expensive suits, not from Freeport, stopped by the mayor's office about ten minutes after you left for the hospital," she said. "And I'm certainly not telling you that the mayor has been pacing back and forth, trying to get hold of you."

"Yeah, I didn't answer his call," Bradley admitted.

"And I didn't tell you that I happened to call his secretary and she happened to look at the cards one of the suits handed the mayor and it was from a pharmaceutical company in Milwaukee."

He smiled. He couldn't help himself. "So, Dorothy, have you ever thought about becoming a detective on the force?" he asked.

"No, it's much more exciting just being your assistant," she replied evenly.

"Well, I didn't tell you that I'm heading over to Mary's office," he said. "And I also didn't tell you that Alex Boettcher is already involved with the case and he's meeting me there too."

He could hear her sigh of relief over the phone line, and it warmed his heart. "Thanks, Dorothy," he said. "It's nice to know you have my back."

She chuckled softly. "Even when I don't, right?"

"Exactly," he said. "Thanks again."

He disconnected the phone and turned down Main Street towards Mary's office. "Suits," he said aloud. "Well, that makes this a bit more interesting."

Chapter Forty-one

Bradley parked behind Alex, and they both exited their vehicles at the same time. Alex waited for Bradley.

"I got an interesting phone call," Bradley said. "Some representatives from a pharma company in Milwaukee stopped by City Hall about ten minutes after I left. The Mayor has been looking for me ever since."

Alex shook his head. "Don't you just love politics?" he replied sarcastically.

They entered Mary's office, and she stood and walked over to greet them.

Alex enfolded her in a hug. "You look amazing," he said.

"Thank you," she replied with a smile. "You don't look too bad yourself."

Alex looked over his shoulder to Bradley. "If I had only met her first," he said.

Bradley grinned. "You did meet her first," he said. "She was just so not interested."

Shocked, Alex turned back to Mary. "I don't believe that," he said. "Did we meet before you met Bradley?"

"No," she replied. "We did not." She glanced to Bradley and shook her head. "But, even though you are a very handsome man, my heart was only meant for Bradley."

Sighing dramatically, he walked across the room, slipped off his overcoat and hung it on a coat rack. "I suppose I can see that," he said, walking over to Mary's desk. "And someday I'll be able to reconcile myself to it."

Mary laughed. "Yeah, I bet your heart's broken," she teased as she walked over to her chair and sat down. Then she looked up. "Oh, I'm sorry. Can I get you anything? Water? Soda?"

"I'll get it," Bradley offered before Mary could stand up again. He walked to the back of her office and opened the small fridge. "What would you like?"

"Water for me," Mary said.

"Me too," Alex added, taking a seat across from her.

With waters in hand, Bradley came back across the room, shrugged off his jacket and sat down.

"So, what do you have?" Mary asked.

"A very nervous CEO who has been receiving payments for space that hasn't been used for more than twenty years," Alex began. "And a nurse who wants us to believe that she didn't know the drugs she was giving the children caused side effects."

"But asked to have her lawyer present the moment she walked into the CEO's office," Bradley added.

"I actually feel sorry for her," Mary said. "She's been living with this hanging over her head for years, just waiting for the other shoe to drop."

"We have data, thanks to the helpful CEO, that records payments all the way back to the nineties," Bradley said. "For the rental of the back unit."

"Wow. Good work," Mary said.

"So, what do you have?" Alex asked.

"I went over to the county offices, and Linda helped me find an old DCFS file that was labeled the Baker's Dozen," Mary said.

"Baker's Dozen?" Alex asked.

"That's what the children said there were called," Mary replied.

Alex paused for a long moment and finally spoke. "The dead children told you what they were called," he said slowly.

"Well, not actually," Mary replied.

Alex exhaled evenly and nodded. "Okay, good," he said.

"They told Clarissa and Maggie what they were called," she added. "We've only interacted with two of them."

Alex sat back in his chair. "You know this..." he waved his hands in the air, "whole dead people talking thing is not admissible in court."

Mary smiled widely. "Really? You don't think so?" she asked.

Closing his eyes, Alex shook his head. "I'm sorry. Of course you know," he said. "Tell me what you learned from them, and I'll just sit here and pretend I'm not totally freaked out."

"The children all had AIDS," Mary said. "They were given drugs that made them hurt even more. Then everyone left them alone."

"Wait! They abandoned the children and locked them in to die?" Alex asked.

"No," Mary replied. "I think the children died, one after the other, but their spirits didn't leave. So once all of them died, they closed up the study and locked the unit."

"With all the paperwork and samples still left behind," Bradley added.

Alex turned to Bradley. "Wait. What? You have records and samples?"

"We got into the unit last night," Bradley explained. "And they had a room behind the nurses station that held the information."

"How did you get in?" Alex asked.

"To the unit or the door behind the nurses station?" Mary asked pointedly.

He stared at her for a moment. "The one I want to know about," he said.

She smiled. "Maggie found a set of keys at the nurses station when she and Clarissa were in there," she said. "She put them in her pocket, and one of them opened the door."

Alex sat for a moment, deciding if he really wanted to know about the other door. Finally, with a sigh, he asked, "Okay, how did you get into the unit?"

"Jack opened the door for us," Bradley said with a gleam of humor in his eye.

"And Jack is..." Alex asked.

"One of the dead children," Mary said. Then her smile faded. "Alex, he was only six when he died. He was the youngest."

"I'm sorry, Mary," Alex said. "I'm going to do everything I can to make it right."

Chapter Forty-two

Margaret finished her visit with Stanley and Rosie, a smile still on her face as she walked to the elevators. Those two were such a hoot! And they were still the cutest newlyweds, so much love and understanding. She pressed the down button and waited for a moment until the elevator door opened. Then she stepped inside and stared at the control panel for a long moment.

Why in the world did she have an almost overwhelming feeling to press three?

Being too Irish to not heed a sign, Margaret pressed three and prayed silently that it was the right thing to do.

The elevator door slid open, and Margaret hit the stop button before she stepped out into the dim hallway. She slowly moved forward, one step at a time, studying either side of the lobby. The abandoned nurses station was dark and filled with shadows in the late afternoon light. Suddenly, an overhead light started to slowly sway.

"This is not a good idea," Margaret decided, backing towards the elevator. But too late, she heard the bell ring behind her and the door slide closed.

Turning, she faced the nurses station. "Well, that was a neat trick," she said aloud. "I hit the stop button, so you must have pulled it back out. What is it you want?"

A door to her left, the door to the supply room, creaked open slowly. Margaret shook her head. "I wasn't born yesterday," she said. "I won't be going into that room so you can lock me in."

Hide!

The whispered command chilled Margaret to the bone. "What?" she stammered, her voice catching in her throat.

Hide!

Only then did Margaret hear the footsteps coming down the hall from the darkened unit. Mustering her courage, she slipped inside the supply room and pulled the door to the edge of the doorframe but didn't close it all the way.

She breathed slowly and softly as her heart pounded against her chest. What in the world was she doing here? She was a grandmother, not a private investigator.

"We should have closed this place down years ago," one angry male voice said.

"We had to wait until the statute of limitations had expired," another male voice, weak and apologetic, replied.

"Well, we're not going to be able to do that, are we?" the first voice answered.

"All we know is that the sensor was activated," the second man said. "It could have been a maintenance person."

"They don't have keys," the first man said.

"They could have picked the lock," the second man argued. "Looking for a place to take a nap."

"Do you really think anyone in their right mind would take a nap in that unit?" the first man roared. "The place gives me the creeps."

"We just don't know what happened," the second man said. "We just have to be calm and reasonable about this whole thing."

"Do you know what could happen to our company if someone uncovers the fact that we were testing non-FDA-approved drugs on minors?" the first man asked, his voice cold and clipped. "Not just bankruptcy. Prison. I don't want to go to prison."

There was silence for a long moment.

"I didn't know they weren't approved," the second man choked. "You never…"

"We didn't want to spend the money on the approval process until we knew they would work," the first man said. "These kids were going to die anyway…"

"When does the statute of limitations end?" the second man asked, his voice shaking. "When will we be safe?"

"End of this month," the first man replied. "So nothing, and I mean nothing, can go wrong. And we really need to tie up any loose ends. Understand?"

"Yeah," the second man whispered. "I understand."

The elevator door signal rang, and Margaret heard the doors slide open. Even though she heard them step inside the elevator and heard the doors close, she still waited for several minutes before working up the nerve to peek out of the door.

She nearly gasped aloud when she saw one of the men was still standing in the hallway. She stumbled backwards and fell against a shelf in the supply room, knocking a pile of sheets onto the ground. Whomp! The sound wasn't loud, but it was noticeable.

"Who's there?" she heard the voice of the first man. The angry one. She heard the click of shoes against the tile floor. He was coming in her direction.

She slowly moved back into the dark, narrow aisle of the storeroom. Lightly touching the sides to guide herself in the dark, she placed her feet down carefully so she didn't make another sound.

Please, she prayed. *Please don't let him find me.*

Suddenly she heard a loud clatter coming from the hallway. She froze and waited.

"What the hell?" the first man screamed.

The elevator signal rang, and she heard footsteps running away from the storeroom to the elevator. The signal of the door closing sounded, and there was silence.

Margaret put her hand on her chest to calm her heart and finally, slowly moved forward in the room. She peeked out the door and, with a sigh of relief, found that the space in front of the elevator doors was empty. Then she looked over to the nurses station and saw the overhead light swinging vigorously back and forth.

She smiled and nodded in the direction of the light. "Thank you," she whispered. "I'll be sure to let the others know what I learned."

Chapter Forty-three

"Carol Ford?" Alex asked. "Why do I know that name?"

"You know, if I had a dollar for every time someone said that today," Mary said. "Carol Ford used to work for DCFS, and she was convicted of embezzling funds."

Alex nodded. "Yes, that's it," he said. "They found thousands in her checking account. She denied knowing anything about it."

Mary sat back in her chair. "Well, that's interesting," she said. "She was the caseworker for all of the kids that were part of the study."

"So, she could have been paid off and someone discovered it," Bradley suggested.

"Or she found out what they were doing, and they got her out of the way," Mary added. "Jerry says that her sentence was over the top."

"Jerry?" Alex asked.

"Jerry Wiley, the editor of the Freeport Republic," Mary said.

"Wiley has a first name?" Alex asked, astonished. "Okay, well, Wiley knows his stuff. What did she get?"

"Thirty years," Mary said.

"Thirty for embezzling?" Alex exclaimed. "That's crazy. She won't get out…"

"Until next year," Mary said. "She's served twenty-nine years."

"She didn't get parole?" Bradley asked.

Mary shook her head. "No, no parole," she said. "I haven't had a chance to look at her records…" She looked at Alex and raised an eyebrow.

"Yeah, I'll get on that right away," he replied with a smile. "But, I think I'll want to review them first."

Mary nodded. "When can we get in to see her?" she asked.

"How does tomorrow sound?" he asked.

"Sounds great," Mary said. "Sounds like she might be holding the key to this whole thing."

"We should also look at the names of the people on the parole board for her," Bradley said, "and see if any of them have been associated with the hospital."

Mary turned from Alex to Bradley. "Okay, sorry, you're going to have to explain that one to me," she said.

"Unless she was a terrible prisoner, and I would have heard about that," Alex said, "there is no way she shouldn't have been able to knock at least half of the time off her sentence. She wasn't dangerous. She wasn't a repeat offender. This was a white collar crime. So, someone wanted her to stay in prison."

Mary nodded in understanding. "Oh, because she had information," she said, "they wanted to hush her up."

"Potentially," Bradley said. "That's the angle I want to explore."

"Okay, yeah, let's explore that angle," Alex agreed. "But let's first talk about the men in black. And what we're going to do about them."

"Men in black?" Mary asked. "What did I miss?"

The bell over her office door rang, and all three of them turned to see Margaret rush into the office. "Oh, good," she breathed. "I'm so glad you're all here."

Mary pushed herself out of her chair and hurried forward. "Mom, are you okay?"

Margaret shook her head. "No. No indeed," she said. "I'm not okay. And I really need to talk about it."

Bradley and Alex were both immediately at her side, helping her into a chair.

"Just sit down, Margaret," Bradley said. "And take a couple of deep breaths."

"Well, I'll sit," Margaret agreed. "But I need to tell someone before I explode."

"What, Mom?" Mary asked. "What do you need to tell us?

"I need to tell you about what happened to me at the hospital."

Chapter Forty-four

"Are you sure this is what you heard?" Alex asked after Margaret had relayed the conversation she overheard while she was in the supply room.

"Young man," Margaret said, "I not only have been married to a police officer for more than 50 years. I have also raised four police officers. I understand how important it is to ensure someone's testimony is offered as truthfully and clearly as possible. I am sure this is what I heard."

Alex nodded. "I believe you, Mrs. O'Reilly," he said. "And, for the record, I didn't doubt you for a moment."

She smiled at him. "Thank you, Alex," she replied. "But now what are we going to do?"

"Well, first," Alex said, looking at Bradley, "I'm going to need those drug samples and the notebooks you rescued from the hospital."

"No problem," Bradley said. "I can bring those to your office after this meeting."

Alex was silent for a moment, and then he shook his head. "No, why don't you bring them to my house instead," he said. "Let's be careful until we know who our friends are."

"And who our enemies are," Mary added. "This is crazy. Why would they give drugs to children that hadn't been cleared by the FDA?"

"Because it can cost billions of dollars for research and development to get drugs to a point where they can be evaluated by the FDA," Alex said.

"Billions?" Mary asked, astonished.

"Yes. With a B," Alex replied.

"That's a huge budget," Bradley said. "And if someone were circumventing the budget in order to line their own pockets..."

"You don't think the company itself did this?" Margaret asked.

"I'm not sure," Bradley said. "But it doesn't make sense that a company would risk everything just to cut a few corners, especially back then when the FDA was eager to approve drugs that were AIDS related."

"That makes it even more dangerous," Alex said. "One person, or a small group of people, can get frightened into doing stupid things."

"So, they're tying up loose ends," Mary said. "That's what Ma heard them say. I wonder if they cleaned out all the rest of the samples and data when they were in the unit this afternoon."

"You're not going to find out," Alex said.

"Excuse me?" Mary asked, a little annoyed that he had shut her down so quickly.

"If they have a sensor that notifies them when people enter the unit, the more times we go in and out the more frightened and dangerous they become," he explained. "If we already have samples with dates and records with dates, we don't need anything else."

She took a long breath. "Okay, that makes sense," she agreed. "But there's got to be something else in that unit that we haven't discovered yet."

"Why do you say that?" Margaret asked.

"If they took the rest of the records and the samples," Mary said, "why do they have to demolish the area early? If it's cleaned out, why attract more attention to the space?"

Alex unfolded himself from his chair and slowly paced the room. "You're right," he said. "There's something there. But I don't want to risk—"

"The elevator," Margaret interrupted.

"What?" Alex asked.

"The day I was trying to get down to the girls on the third floor, the nurse said the elevator had been acting up," Margaret said. "Something with the wiring. If we were able to cut the power to that area of the hospital and say it was because they were repairing the elevator, the sensor would be shut down, wouldn't it?"

"If the sensor was installed in the nineties, it would not be on battery or solar power," Bradley said. "It would rely on power from the hospital."

"But how do we know which section the unit is powered from?" Alex asked.

Bradley thought about Mel and nodded. "I know a guy."

Chapter Forty-five

"It's Friday, right?" Mary asked as she walked into the house and sat on the nearest chair, too tired to even take her coat off.

"No, it's only Tuesday," Clarissa grumbled, her head resting in her hands as she watched a show on the television. "And it's boring."

Margaret came in from the kitchen. "How did the rest of your day go?" she asked.

Mary sighed. "I spent the rest of the afternoon going through the file on the children," she said. "I made a lot of notes, but nothing seemed to be significant."

"Did you hear that, Clarissa?" Margaret said. "Your mother has been working on the ghost children in the hospital case."

Clarissa shrugged in response. "Great," she said indifferently. "At least they have friends."

"You could have a friend too," Mary said, "if you would walk over to Maggie's and apologize."

Clarissa whipped around quickly to face her mother. "I didn't do anything wrong!" she exclaimed.

"Perhaps not," Mary agreed. "But you made Maggie sad, even if it was unintentional. So you could tell her that you are sorry you made her sad."

Clarissa turned back to the television. "She should apologize to me first," she said. "She was the one who called me a big baby. She should say sorry."

Mary nodded, too tired to continue with the argument. "You're probably right," she said, pushing herself out of the chair to hang her coat up. "But then you need to decide if you would rather be lonely or right."

Clarissa didn't respond, and Mary followed her mother back into the kitchen.

"Was I ever..." Mary began.

"Yes, you were that stubborn," Margaret said with a smile. "And you were about the same age. But, eventually you came around."

Mary climbed onto a barstool, picked up a carrot and took a bite. "And, obviously, you survived," she remarked.

Margaret laughed. "Aye, I did," she agreed. "But I wasn't pregnant when you were Clarissa's age."

Sighing, Mary nodded. "I just want to be sure I'm not reacting because I'm pregnant and tired," she said. "I want to be fair."

Margaret chopped several stalks of celery as she spoke. "What I heard out there was more than fair," she said. "Clarissa needs to humble herself a little and approach Maggie."

"That might take a while," Mary said.

"The only one she's hurting is herself," Margaret replied. "I watched her get off the bus. Maggie was all smiles and laughter, playing around with her brothers. Clarissa was sullen and angry. Your poor door took quite a bit of abuse."

"Well, hopefully the door won't have to be abused for too much longer," Mary replied. She inhaled deeply. "Everything smells delicious. What are you making?"

Margaret smiled. "Homemade chicken soup with dumplings," she said. "It seemed like that kind of day."

Mary leaned forward and placed a kiss on her mother's soft cheek. "You have just brightened my whole day," she said. "What can I do to help?"

Margaret picked up the celery and placed it in a cast iron pan to sauté. "You can go upstairs and take a nap before dinner," she said.

"Ma, I want to help," Mary argued.

"You and Mikey have had a full day," Margaret stated in a tone that brooked no argument. "You go and put your feet up for a little while. Dinner will be ready in an hour."

"Thank you," Mary said, more grateful than she wanted to admit. "Call me if you need me."

"I will, darling," Margaret replied with a tender smile. "Go. Sleep."

Chapter Forty-six

The fire crackled in the fireplace, and soft music floated in the air. Mary sighed contentedly and lifted another piece of popcorn into her mouth. "This is just perfect," she said. "I feel so relaxed."

"Good," her mother said, sitting in the recliner near her. "I'm so glad to hear that. You need to relax."

"Any more relaxed and I'd be asleep," she laughed. "So, Clarissa, how's your paper going?"

Clarissa sighed dramatically. "Fine, I guess," she said. "It supposed to be about my Christmas vacation, but since Maggie isn't my friend anymore, I can't talk about her." She threw her pencil onto the coffee table. "I just can't write about anything."

Mary looked over at Bradley, who was sitting behind Clarissa, and he rolled his eyes. "Well," he said, trying to be patient. "You could write about Grandpa Stanley and his time in the hospital."

"I guess," she said as she picked up her pencil again, and with her head leaning against her other hand, she started to write.

"So, what's your day like tomorrow?" Margaret asked.

"I'm going into the office again," Mary said, "if that's fine with you."

"That's perfect," Margaret said. "I was going to spend the day making up casseroles for your freezer."

"Why does our freezer need casseroles?" Clarissa asked.

"Grandma is going to make some dinners and freeze them so we can eat them later," Mary explained. "When she isn't here with us anymore."

Clarissa looked over her shoulder at Margaret. "Don't you want to stay forever?" she asked.

Margaret leaned forward and hugged her granddaughter. "Oh, darling, I would love that," she said. "But eventually I do have to go home and take care of Grandpa."

"Fine," Clarissa sighed. "I guess you should take care of Grandpa."

"Why thank you, dear," Margaret said. "I'm sure he would be very happy to hear you say that."

Bradley coughed to cover his laughter and then shook his head. "Mary," he said, trying to change the subject, "what are you doing at your office?"

"The funniest thing happened today," she said. "Mike stopped by my office and, among other things, suggested that I not renew my lease for my office."

"For heavens sake, why not?" Margaret asked. "It's such a nice place."

Mary shrugged. "I have no idea," she said. "He was fairly closed-lipped about the reason. But…"

"But when an angel suggests something," Bradley inserted, "it's wise to listen."

Mary nodded. "That's what I thought too," she agreed. "So, I'm going to start going through things and packing up."

"Where are you going to work if you don't work there?" Clarissa asked.

"I'm not sure," Mary replied. "But, I was going to take some time off work when Mikey was born anyway. So, I guess I can figure it out then."

"That's a good idea," Margaret agreed. "Once a wee baby comes into a home a lot of things change."

"We could move," Clarissa said.

"What?" Bradley asked.

"We could move," she repeated. Then her voice trembled. "Because it's not like I have any friends that live close by or anything."

"Clarissa," Mary said sympathetically.

Brushing some tears from her cheeks, Clarissa shook her head. "I'm going upstairs," she announced, picking up her notebook and pencil. "I'm tired."

"Sweetheart," Mary said, pushing herself up.

"No, it's okay," Clarissa replied, jumping up and hurrying to the stairs. "I just have to go. Goodnight."

She dashed up the stairs and slammed her bedroom door.

"Poor thing," Mary said.

"Poor door," Bradley added.

"Just wait until she's a teenager," Margaret said with a shake of her head.

Chapter Forty-seven

Mary leaned back in her chair and tried to stretch to get the kinks out of her lower back. She had been bent over, as far as she could bend over, sorting through file drawers and deciding the things she could throw away and the things she needed desperately to keep. She looked at the note Bradley had written her on their first official date. It was a torn piece of paper with a messy note written in marker. She thought about it for another moment and sighed. "Keep pile."

She was about to reach for another manila folder when the bell over the door rang. "Thank you," she gushed, turning in her chair with a smile that disappeared when she saw Alex and Bradley standing just inside the door.

"What?" she asked immediately, frightened by the looks on their faces.

"How many people know you're working on this case?" Alex asked.

Mary felt a chill slip down her spine. "No one," she said slowly. "Well, Linda, but no one else. Why?"

Bradley walked over to her and knelt next to her chair. "Carol Ford is dead."

"What?" she exclaimed.

"I got a call from the jail this morning," Alex said. "They found her in her cell, unresponsive."

"How…how did she die?" Mary asked slowly, her breath shallow.

"We don't know yet," Alex said. "I've requested an autopsy."

"But you don't think it was from natural causes, do you?" Mary asked, knowing the answer before she asked the question.

Alex sat down in the chair across from her and shook his head. "I think it's a little too coincidental," he said. "And, the comment they made yesterday about tying up loose ends…"

"She was a loose end," Mary said. She closed her eyes in self-disgust. "Why didn't I think of that?"

"None of us thought of that," Bradley said. "I don't think any of us realized the length they would go to in order to protect themselves."

"A billion dollars is a lot of money," Mary said.

Alex released a long breath and stood up. "Well, they did protect themselves," he said. "The greatest threat to them has died along with any information she might have been able to share with us. We'll never know now."

Mary and Bradley looked at each other. "Well, that's not necessarily true," Mary said.

"Are you doing the creepy ghost thing again?" Alex asked.

Mary shrugged. "It's not creepy when it's just a part of who you are," she replied. "I can see and talk to ghosts. If you want to get information from Carol Ford, I might be able to get it."

"Might?" Alex asked.

"Well, if she didn't have any unfinished business here on earth, she might have already moved on," Mary said. "So, then we're out of luck."

"She was jailed on trumped-up charges, and then she was killed just before she was going to finally be released," Alex said. "I would say she'd have some unfinished business."

"That would be my guess too," Mary agreed. "How soon can we get in there?"

"Does the body need to be there?" he asked.

Mary shook her head. "No, her spirit has already separated from her body," she said.

Alex exhaled a sigh of relief. "Good. Because that would have been creepy," he said. "So, what do you need? Does it need to be, like, midnight? Do we need candles?"

Mary looked at Bradley and rolled her eyes. Then she turned back to Alex. "We need a blood sacrifice," she said sarcastically.

"Are you kidding me?" Alex exclaimed.

"Yes," Mary replied. "We just need to be able to access her cell without anyone disturbing us."

"Because it will bother the spirit, right?" Alex asked.

"No, because some people get weirded out when they find out I can see ghosts," Mary replied pointedly. "So, I don't like that information to get out too much."

Alex had the decency to look slightly embarrassed. "Yeah, I can see that," he said. "I'll set up the time at the jail. In the meantime, you might want to call Linda and warn her not to talk about things."

"I will," Mary replied. "And I'll call Ma so she is aware too."

Chapter Forty-eight

Mary pulled into her driveway and was surprised that there were several cars already there. She quickly unbuckled her seatbelt, grabbed her purse and her briefcase, and hurried to the front door.

Thinking about the information Alex had shared with them that morning, she was picturing her mother facing down the goons from the pharmaceutical company with only a spatula and paring knife. She grabbed the doorknob and pushed the door open, lunging inside. "Mom," she called, panic overcoming common sense. "Are you—"

"Mary?" her mother called from the kitchen. "I thought you were going to be at your office today."

Her mother walked into the living room followed by Rosie and Katie.

"What are you…" she started as she continued into the house. When she happened to sniff the air, Mary froze in the hallway as her olfactory senses went on sudden overload. She breathed in the amazing smells emanating from the kitchen.

"What smells amazing?" she finally asked.

Margaret chuckled and hurried forward to greet her daughter. She hugged Mary and then took her purse and briefcase and set them on the side table. "Well, we were going to surprise you," Margaret said. "But since you're here, you might as well join us."

"Join you?" Mary asked, slipping off her coat and hanging it in the closet.

"We're making you freezer meals," Rosie said, stepping forward and giving Mary another hug. "It was Margaret's idea."

"And a brilliant idea," Katie agreed, also giving Mary a hug. "There's nothing better than knowing there's food in the house when you bring a new baby home."

"This is so nice of all of you," Mary said, tears filling her eyes. "I don't know what to say."

"Don't say a word," Rosie advised. "Just come into the kitchen and visit with us while we cook."

Mary shook her head. "I can't just sit and do nothing," Mary said. "I can help."

Katie put her arm around Mary's shoulders and led her forward into the kitchen. "You should really not argue with us," she said, guiding Mary to one of the barstools. "Once Mikey is born, your life will be changed forever, and you will look back on this day and say, 'I'm so glad they made me just sit and watch.'"

Rosie sat down and started peeling potatoes. Katie went over to the other side of the counter and continued to chop vegetables while Margaret stirred a pot on the stove.

Mary shrugged. "I'm just having a baby," she said. "It's not going to be that different."

The three other women looked at each other and burst out in laughter. "Oh, honey," Rosie said. "Welcome to the Mom's Club."

Katie nodded. "The exclusive club where you never get enough sleep and can't go to the bathroom by yourself," she began.

"Won't eat hot food for years because you're helping everyone else," Margaret continued. "And all of your clothes will begin to have interesting stains on them."

Rosie chuckled. "I remember a favorite sweater that I finally had to throw away because of all the snot stains."

Mary shuddered. "Snot stains?"

"Yes, that's when your children pretend they want to hug you," Katie explained. "But all they really want to do is wipe their drippy noses on your clothing." She paused and smiled. "It's adorable."

"But Mikey won't be doing that for years," Mary said. "He'll just be a sweet little baby when I bring him home."

"With built-in, projectile-enhanced weaponry," Katie said and the other two women nodded in agreement.

"What?" Mary asked.

"I still remember the time when Sean was a wee babe," Margaret said, turning from the stove for a moment. "We were getting ready for church. Your father was already dressed, and Sean was in the cutest little romper. I'd finally taken a moment to run to the bathroom and do my hair when your father called out that Sean was making grunting sounds." She laughed softly and shook her head. "He would have such a time with his bowels, grunting like a wee pig and turning red."

She stirred the pot again, then continued. "I called from the bathroom that I would be there in a moment," she recalled. "But your father, being the man he is, decided that he could take care of it on his own. Not more than a minute had passed when I heard a scream coming from the bedroom. I dropped the curling iron and rushed in."

"What happened?" Mary asked.

"The walls, the bed, the floor and your very own father were covered with a light brown spray of baby poop," Margaret replied, shaking her head. "I was amazed at the distance, over four feet in some spots." Margaret turned to Mary. "Your brother had amazing sphincters. And we had to get your father a new suit."

"He shot poop across the room?" Mary asked. "Babies do that?"

"I remember the time Andy shot pee from the couch across the room into Clifford's soda glass," Katie laughed. "Not only distance, but precision."

Katie picked up the bowl of chopped vegetables and poured them into the pan Margaret was stirring.

"Across the room?" Mary asked.

"Aye," Margaret said. "You'll learn soon enough to always have a diaper ready when you're changing them. Never give them a chance to feel the breeze of an open room. They'll take advantage every time."

Mary nodded. "I can handle this," she said with assurance. "I'm a black belt. I can swap diapers with no problem."

"Well, you know," Rosie said. "Those first couple of days, you're not moving as quickly as you'd like."

Katie shook her head. "Not days, weeks," she said with a groan of remembrance. "I couldn't sit in a regular chair for weeks."

"Wait. Why?" Mary asked, looking around at her friends, panic in her eyes.

Margaret walked over to Mary and patted her hand. "Don't worry, darling," she said. "It's all part of the wonder and mystery of giving birth."

"Yeah, you wonder how you ever got yourself in this situation, and the mystery is how siblings are ever born," Katie chuckled.

Rosie laughed. "I remember my dear, first husband holding our little girl in the delivery room, the glow of a new birth in his eyes," she said. "I was having sixteen stitches sewn into my nether regions, so I wasn't glowing quite as much. He smiled down at me and suggested we do this again, soon." She paused, her eyes sparkling with mirth. "I admit I'm not proud of my response. And my doctor assured us that my suggestion was probably not anatomically possible."

"Women should not be held accountable for what they say during childbirth," Katie added. Then she turned to Mary. "And no matter how much someone suggests it, never have someone videotape the birth."

"Aye," Margaret said. "Giving birth is miraculous. It's amazing and it's fulfilling. But there is no way on God's green earth that it's pretty."

"And, quite frankly, what are you going to do with a video like that?" Rosie asked. "I never could understand it. Have a party so all your friends can see you exposed to the world? I don't think so. And don't think your children want to see the miracle of their own birth. It embarrasses them enough to know that their parents actually participated in sex. They certainly don't want to see the results."

"But in all the movies…" Mary began.

"In all the movies the moms leave the hospital in the jeans they wore before they were pregnant," Katie said laughing, with the other two women joining in.

"That doesn't happen either?" Mary asked.

The laughter stopped immediately, and the three women looked at Mary, her eyes wide with fear and her face slightly blanched. Margaret turned off the heat under the pot and shook her head. "Ladies, I believe it's time for a cup of tea and a little intervention."

She walked around the counter and led Mary towards the living room and got her settled on the couch. "Now, the first thing you must remember is that giving birth is a miracle," Margaret said.

"Exactly," Katie added. "The feeling you have when you hold that baby in your arms for the first time is unimaginable."

"But," Rosie added. "With everything worth having, there's some, er, uncomfortable moments you'll experience."

Mary looked at each of the women sitting around her, women who were such an important part of her life, women who she trusted with all her heart. "But it's worth it, right?" she asked, her hands resting on her belly.

They all smiled, and in that moment, she could see the memories of their own miracles reflect on their faces. "Yes," Margaret whispered, wiping away a tear. "It is. More than I could ever describe."

Mary sighed and smiled back at them. "Well, that's a relief," she said. "Because it's pretty much too late to change my mind."

Chapter Forty-nine

The next morning, Bradley drove Mary to the county jail on the outskirts of town. They parked in the visitors parking lot and then met Alex at the door.

"Are you still okay doing this?" he asked.

She nodded. "Yes, I'd like to at least try and give her some peace," she replied.

They walked into the front lobby and were met by a guard.

"The Sheriff said you needed to look at one of the cells," the guard said. "Carol Ford's cell."

Alex nodded. "Yeah, it's just routine," he replied easily.

Mary studied the large man. "Did you know Carol?" she asked.

"Yeah, I did," he said, his tone clipped.

"What did you think about her?" she asked.

"Why? Is this for some report?" he asked.

Mary shook her head and placed her hand on the guard's arm. "No, no report," she said. "I was reading some information about her, and it seemed like she was a woman who really cared about people."

The guard sighed and nodded, his eyes filling with tears. "Yeah, she was good," he said, his voice hoarse. "She was a Christian, you know, a real Christian."

Mary nodded. "She lived her religion, not just talked about it?"

"She shouldn't have been here," he said. "Someone screwed her real good. But since she was here, she was like everyone's auntie. Everyone asked her for advice."

"Did she give you good advice?" Mary asked.

"She saved my marriage," he said, "made me a better man for knowing her."

"Well, I'm very sorry I didn't get to meet her," Mary said. "I missed out."

He nodded. "Yes, you did," he said. Then he took a deep breath and nodded. "Come on, we can go down now."

They followed him through the security gates and into the main section of the jail. Then he led them through the main section and downstairs to private cells.

"Why was she down here?" Alex asked. "This is isolation. She wasn't a danger to anyone."

The guard nodded. "Yeah, that's a good question," he said. "A real good one."

He unlocked a small cell and stepped back. "This is it," he said.

"We have to run some tests and do some analysis," Alex said. "Can you come back for us in about fifteen minutes?"

"You want me to leave you alone in a cell?" he asked, surprised.

"Just for a little while," Alex said. "Too many people can contaminate the sample."

The guard shrugged and nodded. "Okay, you should be safe down here," he said. "I'll be back in

269

fifteen. You need me any sooner, just call on that emergency phone on the post in the hallway."

"Thank you," Alex replied. "I will."

The guard turned and left them.

"He's a good man." The woman's voice had Mary turning towards the cell.

"He spoke very highly of you," Mary replied.

"Wait! What? Is it happening?" Alex asked.

Mary glanced over and quickly shook her head to silence him.

"Oh. Sorry," he replied, stepping away from the cell. Then he turned to Bradley. "What do we do now?"

"We wait," Bradley said. "And listen."

Chapter Fifty

"My name is Mary," Mary said to the ghost sitting on the bunk in the cell.

"I'm Carol," the distinguished, African American woman said. "Carol Ford."

"Carol, are you aware that…"

"That I'm dead?" Carol asked with a bit of humor in her voice. "Oh, yes, child. I realized that when I stood up and my body didn't come with my spirit."

"That would have been a little disconcerting," Mary said.

The woman laughed out loud. "Well, to say the least," she replied. "To say the least." She looked at Mary. "Is this your first baby?"

Mary nodded. "I have a nine-year-old stepdaughter," Mary explained, "who I consider to be my child." Mary put her hands on her belly. "But this is the first time I will give birth."

"Well, God bless you," Carol said. "That's just wonderful. A new baby is always a miracle."

Mary nodded. "Yes, it always is," she said. "And babies and children, they have a right to be protected and loved and nurtured."

"Amen," Carol replied. "I couldn't agree more."

"I have a gift. Some may call it a responsibility," Mary explained. "I can see and communicate with spirits—those who are still here on earth because they have unfinished business."

"Is that why I'm still here?" Carol asked.

Mary nodded. "It would seem so," she said. "Or perhaps you're here because of someone else's unfinished business."

"And who would that be?"

"The Baker's Dozen," Mary said.

"Those children? Those poor children are still here?" she asked, aghast.

Mary nodded. "They are still in the hidden unit at the hospital," she explained. "And they're frightened."

272

A translucent tear slipped down Carol's cheek and made a darkened path to her jawbone. "I thought they'd move on," she said. "I thought once their pain had ended…"

"Did you know what they were doing to the children?" Mary asked.

Carol took a shuddering breath, then shook her head. "Not at first," she said. "These poor children were sick. They had all contracted the HIV virus from their mothers who had died from AIDS. They approached us and said that they would be willing to treat the children with cutting-edge treatments—treatments that might cure them. We just had to agree that they could record the children's progress for their study."

"Who is they?" Mary asked.

"Well, the first person to approach me was Dr. Reinsband," she said. "He'd done work with DCFS before, and the children seemed to like him. And it was just a matter of moving the children from pediatrics to this special, new, isolation unit."

"After Dr. Reinsband talked to you, who else met with you?"

"The men from the pharmaceutical company came to see me," she said. "They needed my signature on the paperwork as the guardian ad litem for the children." She closed her eyes in concentration. "Let's see. There was a Hickory. Maybe Joe Hickory. And, another plant name." She smiled at Mary.

"I remembered them as the plant brothers. Now, what was his name?"

She looked up to the ceiling and then nodded. "Ash. That was his name. Simon Ash."

"Okay, Joe Hickory and Simon Ash," Mary repeated, raising her voice slightly so Bradley and Alex could hear clearly, "were the two men from the pharmaceutical company."

"Oh, and the doctor who worked for the company too," she said. "His name was odd. What was it? Claeys. That's it. Dr. Samuel Claeys."

"Dr. Claeys worked for the pharmaceutical company?" Mary exclaimed.

"Claeys worked for them?" Alex repeated. "When was that?"

Carol nodded. "Yes, he was the one that explained how the cutting edge formulations would help the children," she said.

"Do you remember when this all happened?" Mary asked.

Carol nodded. "Yes, spring of 96," she said. "That's when I agreed to let the children participate."

"Spring of 96," Mary repeated. "Dr. Claeys is the CEO for Freeport Hospital now."

Carol shook her head. "Well, that doesn't surprise me," she said. "He seemed like the kind of man who landed on his feet wherever he went."

Chapter Fifty-one

Bradley moved down the hallway a little and pulled out his phone. "Dorothy, it's Bradley," he said. "I need you to run a background check on Dr. Samuel Claeys. I want you to check bank accounts, real estate holdings, investments. I want everything you can give me on this guy. Thanks."

Alex joined him. "Okay, I've got my office running checks on Ash and Hickory," he said. He paused for a moment and shook his head. "Is this for real?"

"Yeah, it's for real," Bradley assured him.

"So, is it like one of those Ouija boards?" he asked. "She gets like messages or feelings?"

Bradley shook his head. "No, she can see Carol Ford," he said. "She is talking to the spirit of Carol Ford."

Alex shook his head. "I have a hard time getting my head around this," he said.

"Yeah, so did I until I saw them too," Bradley said.

Alex looked surprise. "Wait. You can do this paranormal thing too?"

"No, only if I make contact with Mary while she's talking to one of the ghosts," he said.

"Make contact?" Alex asked. "Is that a code word for…"

"Touch her hand or her arm, Alex," Bradley countered. "That's it, Alex."

"Good because, you know, that would have been kind of weird…"

"Alex," Bradley interrupted.

"Yes?"

"Shut up," Bradley said.

Bradley walked back down the hallway to the cell where Mary was still conversing with Carol. Alex followed close behind him.

"Hey, I'm sorry," Alex said. "I didn't mean to be offensive or anything."

"Don't worry about it," Bradley said. Then he turned to Alex and stared at him for a long moment. "Yeah, that might work."

"What?" Alex asked.

But Bradley just walked away from him and into the cell with Mary. He placed his hand on Mary's shoulder, and instantly he could see the woman Mary was conversing with.

Mary smiled up at him then turned back to the ghost. "Carol, this is my husband, Bradley," she said. "He's also the chief of police."

"So, are you going to make those men pay for what they did?" Carol asked him.

He nodded. "Yes, ma'am, I plan on making them pay for a very long time," he replied. Then he looked over his shoulder. "The other man, standing there, his name is Alex Boettcher. He's the Stephenson County District Attorney. He's working on this case too."

"He's the excitable man," Carol replied.

Bradley and Mary both grinned. "Yes. Yes, he is," Mary agreed.

"I wanted to see if Alex might be able to see you too," Bradley said. "I think it might help with this whole process."

Carol nodded. "Well, I'm new at this," she said. "What would you like me to do?"

Bradley turned to Mary.

"I think if you just want Alex to see you, that could be helpful," Mary suggested.

Bradley walked back to Alex. "I want to try something," he said.

Alex shook his head. "Yeah, no, I don't want to be part of some weird experience," he said.

"I think it would give you a better feel for the case," Bradley said. "Give you a chance to interview the witness yourself."

Alex closed his eyes for a moment and shook his head. "I'm going to have nightmares for the rest of my life if I do this," he said.

Bradley smiled. "If I'm lucky," he replied. He grabbed hold of Alex's arm and pulled him into the cell. Then he placed Alex's hand on Mary's shoulder.

"Can you—" Bradley began.

"Holy shit!" Alex exclaimed.

"I think he can see me," Carol laughed. "And I don't think he's too happy about it."

Chapter Fifty-two

"I still can't get over it," Alex said when they were sitting in Mary's office later that morning. "She was right there. Talking and moving, like a real person."

"Well, she is a real person," Mary said. "She just doesn't happen to have a body right now."

He stood up and paced around her office. "This is amazing," he said. "Totally amazing. Can you imagine how easy it would be to solve crimes if you could just talk to the dead guy and ask him who killed him?"

"Well, there are a few problems with that," Mary said with a smile.

Alex turned to her. "What? What could be a problem?" he asked.

She shrugged, and her smile widened. "I don't know, maybe people thinking you're nuts and locking you up for a long, long, long time."

He stopped his pacing and thought about it. "Okay, yeah, that could be a problem," he said. "But, wow! I mean, wow! Talking to her was so…great. What a great lady."

"What a great lady who was murdered," Bradley reminded him.

"Yeah," Alex said, nodding. "Yeah, it's hard to think of her as dead."

"I know what you mean," Mary said. "But we need to solve this case so she can move on."

"Okay, what else did you find out?" Alex asked.

"She decided to visit the children," Mary said. "And she found them all in distress. They told her that they got sick after they took their pills. They didn't want to take their pills anymore."

Mary got up and walked over the refrigerator and pulled out three bottles of water. She tossed a bottle to Bradley and one to Alex. Then she opened her own and took a drink before she continued.

"She asked the nurse about the pills and the side effects. The nurse told her that it was the AIDS, not the pills, that was causing those effects. But, Carol had been with the kids during the first stages of the disease, and they hadn't experienced anything like that. She also thought it was odd that all thirteen children would be experiencing the same side effects so soon after being administered the same drugs."

"Why wasn't the doctor in charge asking those same questions?" Alex asked. "If a social worker could figure it out, why couldn't a physician?"

"That's a really good question," Mary said. "And I think it's one we need to ask Dr. Reinsband when Bradley and I visit him tomorrow."

"We're visiting him tomorrow?" Bradley asked.

"Do you remember Karen Springler?" Mary asked.

He nodded. "Yes, she was the psychologist who worked with Clarissa," he said.

"The nursing home where Dr. Reinsband lives lost their psychologist, so she's doing double duty," she explained. "So, when I told her I needed to meet with Dr. Reinsband, she set it up for tomorrow."

"Did she give you a clue as to his state of mind?" Alex asked.

Mary shook her head. "No, she can't because of the HIPPA laws," she said. "But we should be able to figure it out tomorrow when we meet with him."

"Yeah, and we can solve another puzzle," Alex said.

"What's that?" Bradley asked.

"The doctor registered to Carol Ford's care was Dr. Reinsband," he said.

"What?" Mary asked.

"Interesting, right?" Alex asked. "Carol was on several different medications for her blood pressure and her heart problems."

"Did you check with the jail's dispensary about a change in her medications?" Mary asked.

"Funny thing," Alex said. "The normal pharmacist called in sick, and a temp came in. It's odd with a place as secure as this. You would think they'd have to do a background check or something, but no one seems to know who the temp was."

Bradley pulled out his phone again. "Hey, Sheriff," he said once his call had been answered. "It's Alden. I've got a quick question for you. I've got a friend. We used to be on the force together, and now he's a sheriff in a small town downstate. They're building a prison, not as big as ours, but he's a little overwhelmed. He was asking me how we got our medical staff and our pharmacists."

Bradley nodded slowly. "So, we subcontract with the hospital," he repeated. "Well, that makes a lot of sense. Thanks. Thanks a lot. That's very helpful. Have a good one."

"This really stinks," Mary said.

"Wow, they've got themselves covered all over town," Alex said as he walked over to the door. "I'm going to go over to the morgue and make sure the coroner is still on our side. You guys be careful."

"Alex, who's checking on those samples for us?" Mary asked.

"I've got a friend from Bloomington, Illinois, who's running checks on them," he replied. "Nick Butzirus is a good guy, and I can trust him completely."

"Good," Mary said. "At least Claeys won't be able to mess with that."

"Yeah, but watch your back," Alex said.

"You too," Bradley said. "These guys are playing for keeps."

Chapter Fifty-three

The nursing home was located on Park Avenue across the street from Krape Park. It was the oldest nursing home in the area and the most respected. The stately home had assisted living and full-care suites for its residents. The gathering rooms were bright and sunny, with highly polished woodwork that carried the scent of lemon oil. It was, Mary thought, a place she wouldn't mind spending some time in if she had to.

Dr. Karen Springler met them at the receptionist desk and escorted them to a family meeting room off one of the main gathering rooms.

"Have you ever met Dr. Reinsband?" she asked.

Mary shook her head. "No, I haven't," she said. "But I've heard wonderful things about him. How long has he been here?"

"Almost thirty years," Karen replied. "He was working at the hospital when suddenly he seemed to lose his ability to concentrate, it kept getting worse and he never quite regained his…" She paused, trying to come up with the right word. "Well, I suppose you'll be able to see for yourself."

They walked into the room, and Mary was surprised to see a fairly fit-looking man sitting at a table looking at them. "Hello," he said with a kindly smile. "Do I know you?"

Mary shook her head. "No, you don't," she said. "My name is Mary, and this is my husband, Bradley."

His smile grew. "I thought for sure I knew you," he said. "You look so familiar to me. Were you one of my patients?"

"I don't think so," Bradley said. "But I believe I know some of your patients."

"Do you?" he replied happily. "That's wonderful. Who do you know?"

"Carol Ford," Mary inserted.

His smile turned into a thoughtful frown, and he slowly shook his head. "No. No, I can't say I remember her," he said. "Ford, like the car?"

Bradley nodded. "Exactly."

"No, I've never met her," he said.

"How about Jack Dunne?" Mary asked.

His smile returned. "Little Jack," he said. "What a whippersnapper—so full of life and what a trickster. I remember him gluing all of my tongue depressors together." He chuckled heartily. "How's Jack doing these days?"

"When was the last time you saw Jack?" Bradley asked.

Once again, his smile turned thoughtful as he pondered the question. "Well, as best I recall," he said slowly, "it was back when we were administering this wonder drug to him."

"Wonder drug?" Mary asked.

"Yes. It was the only drug that could fully cure AIDS," he said. "We used it on thirteen children. All wonderful children. Gave them a new lease on life."

"Did you work with the study when the children were given those drugs?" Mary asked.

He stopped and thought about her question for a long moment, then smiled sadly. "I'm so sorry," he said. "But about that time was when my condition appeared. So, I supervised the study, but I relied on my nurse and Dr. Claeys for the details."

He shook his head. "But they were miraculous details," he said. "Simply miraculous."

"Did you sign off on those reports?" Bradley asked.

Dr. Reinsband grinned and then peeked around. "I suppose it doesn't hurt to tell the truth now," he said, lowering his voice to a conspiratorial whisper, "especially since the results were so positive. But, yes, I signed off on everything. I had to, or they wouldn't have been able to bring those drugs to market. And at that time, AIDS was a horrible disease."

"Your condition," Mary asked. "Do you know what caused it?"

He shook his head. "Darndest thing," he said. "All of the sudden, I can't think straight. I can't remember where I put my car, my keys, my house. I can't seem to function for an entire day. Luckily for me, Dr. Claeys was willing to cover for me so I could work long enough to get credit for the study and get the bonus from the pharmaceutical company. That's the only way I could afford to live here."

"If you don't mind me asking," Mary inquired, "how much was your bonus?"

He became thoughtful again. "I can't remember if I had to sign one of those non-disclosure agreements," he said slowly.

"Oh, we won't tell anyone," Mary assured him.

He smiled widely. "Well, it's okay then," he said. "They paid me ten million dollars."

"Ten million?" Bradley asked. "That's a lot of money for a small drug study."

Dr. Reinsband nodded his head in agreement. "I know," he said. "But they make so much money from those drugs, I suppose having those children cured was worth it."

Mary glanced at Bradley and shook her head. "I can't do this," she said.

"What can't you do?" Dr. Reinsband asked.

"Those children did not make it," she said. "They did not get cured. They all died."

"No, that can't be true," he said. "I saw the reports. I signed the reports. The drugs cured them."

"No, the drugs did not cure them," Mary replied. "The drugs were never released to the public because the children died. They all died."

"Did I kill them?" Dr. Reinsband asked anxiously.

Mary shook her head. "No, you didn't," she said. "But they used your name, so the children were afraid of you."

"But…but I would never hurt any children," he said. "I wanted to help them."

"They didn't know that," Mary said. "They still don't know that."

He stared at her. "Are they still there?" he asked, his voice soft.

She nodded. "Yes, they are," she said. "Do you believe in spirits remaining here on earth after death?"

"I have to believe," he replied. "I'm a doctor. I've seen them."

"If you could just come over to the hospital," Mary said, "to that unit…"

He shook his head adamantly. "No. No, I can't leave the nursing home," he said sadly. "My condition has gotten much worse. I can barely remember anything. No, I'm afraid that I'm frightened too."

Mary pulled a card out of her purse and handed it to him. "If you change your mind," she said, "please call me. Those children deserve to know the truth so they can be free."

"Thank you for meeting with us," Bradley said, extending his hand.

"You are welcome," Dr. Reinsband said, shaking his hand and holding on to it. "And, remind me, where did you say we met before?"

"I'm sure it was at the hospital," Bradley said with a sad smile.

"That's it," he said, shaking Bradley's hand again. "I never forget a face."

Chapter Fifty-four

Dr. Karen Springler was waiting for them in the gathering room. "How was your visit?" she asked.

"Could we meet somewhere privately?" Bradley asked.

"Of course," Karen said. "Let's go to my office."

When they were seated in Karen's office, Bradley studied Karen for a moment and finally made up his mind. "Can I trust you?" he asked.

Karen looked a little taken aback. "I beg your pardon?" she asked.

"That sounded rude, and I apologize for that," he said. "But we are working on a case where confidentiality is critical. Not only could evidence be destroyed, but people could die."

"Oh, my goodness," Karen said. "I didn't realize…"

"I just need to be sure which side you are on," Bradley said.

Karen sat back in her chair and smiled softly. "Your wife brought me back from deep depression, and she gave me a gift I can never repay," she said. "I am on your side."

Bradley breathed a sigh of relief and nodded. "Can you tell me who Dr. Reinsband's physician is?"

"Oh, that's easy," Karen said. "Dr. Claeys takes care of him because they are old friends."

"Does anyone check on the medications Dr. Claeys prescribes, or do they just administer them and do what he orders?" Bradley asked.

"Well, I'm assuming that since he's the CEO of the hospital, he doesn't get a lot of pushback from anybody," she said. "Why?"

"We have reason to believe that Dr. Claeys has not been working in the best interests of several of his patients," Bradley said. "It might have been to his advantage to have Dr. Reinsband incapacitated."

Mary turned from Bradley to Karen. "Can medications do that?" she asked. "Can they actually cause a person to have dementia?"

"Well, there is an older class of antidepressants called TCAs that actually caused cognitive impairment that could present itself like dementia. But no one uses those drugs anymore."

"Can you access Dr. Reinsband's prescriptions?" Bradley asked.

She turned toward her computer, then stopped and turned back to them. "I'm sorry," she said. "But I'm breaking every ethical rule I know. I have to know a little more."

Mary nodded. "Do you remember when I was able to speak with your son after he'd died?" she asked.

Karen nodded. "Yes, of course I remember."

"Well, there is a group of thirteen children who died at the hospital," Mary continued. "They were all orphans, and they all had AIDS. A pharmaceutical company told both their DCFS guardian and Dr. Reinsband that they had developed a miracle drug that would cure the children. But, what we've learned is this was a drug that hadn't been approved by the FDA. The company, or at the very least the representatives, was trying to save the cost of getting approval until they could determine if it would actually work. So, the children were used as guinea pigs."

"No, they wouldn't…"

"We have proof," Bradley said. "We have samples of the drugs and records of the side effects."

"Dr. Claeys was with the pharmaceutical company," Mary added. "He was their guy. And he told Dr. Reinsband that all of the children were cured. He had Reinsband sign all of the study documents because they were falsified."

Karen turned in her chair and typed on her keyboard. She clicked on her screen several times, scrolled down a page and gasped softly. Then she turned back to Mary and Bradley. "He has Dr. Reinsband on tricyclic antidepressants. That's probably what's causing his impairment."

"What do you have to do to reverse the effects?" Mary asked.

"Take him off the meds," Karen said.

"You need to do that without alerting Dr. Claeys," Bradley said. "They've already killed one person."

Karen sat motionless for several moments. Then she looked up at Mary and Bradley. "I'm not ashamed to admit that I'm scared to death," she said.

"Good," Bradley said. "You should be."

Her hands shook as she pulled them away from her keyboard and placed them on her lap. "What should I do?"

"You mentioned that no one uses TCAs anymore," Mary said. "So if there is a bottle in the pharmacy, the only one using it would be Dr. Reinsband, right?"

Karen nodded.

"So, can we empty the bottle of those pills and replace them with something else that won't hurt him?" Mary asked.

A smile grew on Karen's face. "Yes. Yes, we can certainly do that," she said. "And I have some vitamin C pills that look just like them."

"Do you need us to help you?" Mary asked. "Create a distraction?"

Karen laughed and shook her head. "No, I will have no problem going to the dispensary and switching out the pills."

She turned to Bradley. "Thank you for trusting me," she said.

Bradley reached over and shook her hand. "Thank you for being on our side."

Chapter Fifty-five

"Do you think Clarissa will be all right?" Mary asked Bradley as they drove down the darkened city streets to the hospital.

"If I say no, does that mean we don't have to go to the birthing class?" Bradley replied with a smile.

"No, we still will have to go, but I'll feel guilty," she said.

He laughed and shook his head. "Clarissa is going to have to work this out on her own," he said. "If anyone, I'd feel sorry for your ma. She's going to have to deal with Clarissa's mood all night."

Looking out the window to the snow-covered lawns, Mary sighed. "I know she's been moody," she said. "But to find out that Maggie and some of the other girls are going to the movies tonight without her? That's hard."

"And it wouldn't have happened if she had just apologized," Bradley reminded her.

"I suppose," Mary said. "It's hard to see her miserable."

Bradley reached over and squeezed Mary's hand. "You're a good mom," he said.

They pulled into the parking lot and found a spot close to the door. As Bradley helped Mary out of the car, he glanced around the parking lot to see a number of other couples doing the same thing. "It looks like a pregnancy convention," he said to Mary.

"Well, they only have this class once a month," she explained. "So it's pretty well attended."

He tucked her arm inside of his and maneuvered her across the slick parking lot with extra care. When they finally reached the sidewalk, he breathed a sigh of relief. "Safe," he whispered.

She smiled up at him. "Thank you," she said. "Now watch me trip on the carpet."

The image of Mary falling rushed through his mind, and he quickly tucked her arm more tightly against his. "Just in case," he said, leading her into the hospital.

They went downstairs to the large meeting room. Normally filled with tables and chairs, the room was nearly empty with only a couple of dozen chairs against one wall. The rest of the floor was open.

"Thanks for coming," the instructor said. "My name is Kara and I will be your instructor for the night. The first thing I need you to do is find a place on the floor to get comfortable."

Mary turned to Bradley. "I think concrete floor and getting comfortable don't really go together," she whispered.

"Well, we have your yoga mat," he whispered back.

"Oh, well then," she grinned. "Big difference."

Bradley rolled out the mat and helped Mary down to the floor. Then he sat down next to her. "How's that?" he asked with a smile. "Comfy?"

"So comfy," she replied.

"If I can have your attention," Kara said sharply.

"Busted," Bradley whispered, and Mary had to clap her hand over her mouth to muffle the laughter.

"The first thing we're going to talk about is what labor and delivery is all about," Kara continued as she turned on the projector and turned down the lights. "So, everyone watch up here. This video will show you giving birth to a baby, up close and personal."

Fifteen minutes later, when the lights went back up, Mary turned a panicked face to Bradley. "Drugs," she said urgently. "No matter what I say during labor, promise me that you will insist on lots of drugs."

He nodded, his own eyes wide with astonishment. "I am so sorry I did this to you," he said softly. "I had no idea..."

"If I can have your attention again," Kara said, looking pointedly at Mary and Bradley. "Let's now talk about breathing."

"I can still breathe," Mary whispered. She inhaled and exhaled several times. "See."

Bradley choked, and Mary's grin widened.

"This breathing helps you relax so your contractions can work with your body," Kara explained. "When you tense your muscles, the contractions can't push the baby down and out. When you relax them, the baby and your contractions work together."

Mary turned to him again. "Drugs," she whispered again.

"Now, I want you all to practice this," Kara said. "Ladies, look into your partner's eyes and breathe. Hee. Hee. Hee. Hee."

Mary looked up into Bradley's eyes and saw the mirth there. "Don't you dare make me laugh," she whispered.

He nodded. "Hee. Hee. Hee. Hee," he repeated.

Her lips trembled, and she shook her head. "Stop it," she whispered urgently.

"Hee. Hee. Hee. Hee," he repeated.

She bit her lower lip. "Hee," she began, but a giggle escaped after it.

"Hee," she tried again, but it was too much. Tears ran down her face as laughter overcame her.

Bradley's laughter joined hers, and soon they were leaning against each other on the floor.

"You have to help me up," Mary finally whispered urgently.

"Why?" Bradley gasped.

"I really have to pee," she said.

Still gasping for air, he helped her up, and they hurried out of the room.

Several minutes later as Bradley punched the elevator button for the fourth floor, he shook his head. "Obviously Kara does not have much of a sense of humor," he said.

"What am I going to tell my mother," Mary asked, "when she finds out I was expelled from my birthing class."

"She'll never find out," Bradley replied with a conspiratorial tone. "And that's why we're going to visit Stanley and Rosie."

"You're brilliant," she replied as they stepped into the elevator together.

"And you're gorgeous," he said, taking her into his arms and kissing her once the doors closed. "And I don't care what Kara says. I think your breathing is sexy."

Chapter Fifty-six

Clarissa sat at the desk in her bedroom not reading the book in front of her. She was just so angry she wanted to throw something, or scream at someone, or something. She sighed. She couldn't yell at Grandma— that would be too rude. And she didn't want to throw something because something else might break, and then she would get in trouble.

Lucky, her kitten, jumped up on the desk and rubbed against Clarissa's arm, purring as loudly as she could. Clarissa picked the kitten up and placed her on the floor. "Go away, Lucky," she said. "I don't want to pet you right now."

"Tough day?"

Clarissa turned around to see Mike standing near the door.

"I don't want to talk about it," she said, turning away from him.

"The only way you can get the emotion out is to share it," he advised.

She turned back to him. "Do you know what Maggie said about you?" she snapped. "She said that you were just my babysitter. That I didn't have special powers like hers, and the only reason I can see you is because I'm a baby and you have to watch over me."

Mike shook his head. "No, that's not—"

"Are you my babysitter?" Clarissa asked pointedly.

"Well, in a way," Mike began. "But it's because your mother…"

"You're my babysitter because of Mary," she accused. "You watch over me because of her?"

"Let me explain, Clarissa," he said. "It's not like that."

"Do any other kids my age have guardian angels?" she asked.

He nodded. "Yeah, sure, all kids your age have guardian angels," he said.

"No, not like that," she interrupted. "Do any kids my age have guardian angels like you are—that appear and talk to them? That get them out of trouble like you do?"

"I don't know," Mike said.

"You're not supposed to lie," Clarissa shouted.

Mike sighed. "Okay, no," he said. "Most kids don't have guardian angels like me. Most kids don't even know they have guardian angels." He smiled at her. "You're special."

She shook her head. "No, I'm not," she said. "I'm just a baby, like Maggie said."

"You're not a baby," Mike insisted.

Clarissa took a deep, shuddering breath and folded her arms across her chest. "I don't need you anymore," she said to Mike.

"What?" Mike felt like he'd been punched in the solar plexus. "You don't know what you're saying."

"I know," she said angrily. "I'm not a baby. I don't need a babysitter. I don't need you anymore."

"Clarissa, once you send me away, I can't come back," he said.

She shook her head. All she could hear was Maggie's voice calling her a baby. "Go away," she whispered. "I don't want you anymore."

Mike nodded, and his eyes glistened with tears. "Goodbye, Clarissa," he whispered. Then he disappeared.

Clarissa stared at the space he'd just occupied and started to sob. "Wait," she screamed. "Wait, I didn't mean it. Mike, come back. I didn't mean it. Mike!"

Chapter Fifty-seven

Mary gasped softly, and Bradley immediately looked over at her. "What's wrong?" he asked.

"I don't know," she said, brushing a tear from her cheek. "Suddenly I feel so sad."

"Pregnancy hormones?" he asked.

She sniffled and shook her head. "I don't know," she replied. "I've never felt like this before."

"How do you feel?" he asked.

"Like I just lost my best friend," she whispered, tears flowing steadily down her cheeks. She grabbed some tissues from the box and blotted her face. "I'm sorry. I don't understand this."

"What would you like me to do?" Bradley asked, concerned and confused.

"Let's go home," Mary said. "I want to be sure everyone's okay."

Bradley turned from the direction of the ice cream shop and headed back to their home. In a few minutes, he pulled into their driveway and helped Mary out of the car.

A sense of dread had been growing in her heart. "We can get our things later," she said. "Let's just go in."

They hurried into the house. "Ma," Mary called, alarm in her voice. "Ma, where are you?"

"Up here," her mother called. "In Clarissa's room."

They both hurried up the stairs and found Margaret sitting on the bed with an inconsolable Clarissa in her arms.

"What happened?" Mary cried, moving to the bed to hug Clarissa.

Clarissa looked up at Mary, her eyes red and swollen from crying. "I'm so sorry," she sobbed. "I'm so sorry."

"Why, sweetheart?" Mary asked. "What did you do?"

"I sent Mike away," she said. "I told him I didn't need him anymore, and I sent him away."

Mary felt like her heart had been ripped out, and she stepped back, sitting on Clarissa's chair. "You did what?" she asked incredulously.

"Maggie said Mike was just a babysitter for me," she said. "And I didn't need a babysitter, so I told him to go away."

Tears slid down Mary's cheeks unchecked. "But he was our family," she whispered. "He was... he was...my best friend."

Clarissa nodded, and her lips trembled with pain. "I'm sorry," she said. "He told me if I sent him away, he could never come back. But I still sent him away because I was mad."

Mary's heart was breaking. She wiped away her tears and shook her head. "I'm sorry," she said. "I can't be in here right now."

She stood up, walked out of the room and down the hallway to her bedroom.

Clarissa looked up at Bradley. "I tried to call him back," she cried. "I tried to say I was sorry."

Bradley shook his head. "I'm sure you did," he said. "But that doesn't change anything right now.

I'm going to go talk to your mother. Why don't you get ready and go to bed."

Bradley walked out of the room, closing the door behind him.

Clarissa looked up at her grandmother. "I tried to get him back, really," she pleaded.

"Well, you've learned a hard lesson today," Margaret said. "When you react in anger and say things that hurt other people, no matter how hard you try, you can never take the words back."

"Do they still love me?" Clarissa asked softly.

Margaret hugged her again. "Aye, of course they do," she said. "They love you no matter what. But you hurt them both, badly. And they need to deal with their grief."

She stood up and stepped away from the bed. "Now do as your father asked," Margaret said. "Get ready and go to bed."

"Can I pray for Mike?" Clarissa asked.

Margaret nodded. "I think that would be a very good idea."

Chapter Fifty-eight

Bradley opened his bedroom door and found Mary lying on the bed, sobbing. He climbed up next to her, pulled her into his arms and held her while she cried.

"She didn't know what she was doing," he said softly.

She nodded against his chest. "I know," she cried. "I know. But he's still gone. And he didn't get to say goodbye."

He rubbed her back and nodded, his own tears flowing freely. "Is there a chance?"

She shook her head. "I don't think so," she said sadly. "Clarissa was kind of the loophole to keep him here, with us. And when she…"

Her voice shook, and she buried her face in Bradley's chest to cry some more.

"When she said she didn't need him, she closed the loophole," he finished for her.

She took a deep breath and wiped her tears with her sleeve. "I didn't mean to upset her," Mary said. "But it just…it just hurt so much."

Bradley reached past her, pulled a handful of tissues from the bedside box and handed them to her. "I think she needs to see that her actions caused you pain," he said. "She needs to be aware that what she did was wrong."

Mary wiped her face and nodded. "But she's also a nine-year-old child who is going to say and do stupid things," she acknowledged. "I remember telling my mother that I hated her when I was her age. I was angry and thoughtless. The pain I saw in my mother's eyes went straight to my heart."

"Did you learn?" he asked.

She nodded. "I never said that to her again," she replied.

"Well, the pain Clarissa saw in your eyes cut her to the heart too," Bradley said. "I think she expected you to say that everything was okay. But you didn't."

Mary shook her head and dabbed the tissue against her eyes. "I couldn't," she said, her voice shaking again. "Because it's not okay. I'm going to miss him so much."

Bradley nodded. "Me too," he said. "He was…" His voice cracked, and he pulled a tissue out for himself. "He was my brother."

Mary reached over and hugged Bradley. "I know," she said. "Mine too."

Chapter Fifty-nine

Bradley leaned over and kissed Mary lightly on the cheek. She slowly opened her eyes and was surprised that the sun was streaming in through the windows. "Good morning," he said. "How did you sleep?"

She stretched slowly and sighed. "Good," she said, and then she remembered. "Mike?"

Bradley shook his head. "No, Clarissa got up early and called for him," he said. "He didn't respond."

"I don't think he could even if he wanted to," Mary said. "Once she sends him away..."

"He has to stay away," Bradley finished. He looked into her eyes. "How are you today?"

She shrugged. "Sad. A little sad," she said. "Well, no, a whole lot sad. But I can handle today."

He kissed her again. "Good, because I have to run into the station for a little bit," he said. "But I should be home by noon. We could do something as a family."

She smiled. "That would be nice," she agreed.

A few minutes later, Mary walked down the stairs, wrapped in her robe. Clarissa was in the living room, staring down at the floor.

"Good morning, Clarissa," Mary said.

Clarissa slowly lifted her head and met Mary's eyes. "I called and called for Mike," she said, shaking her head. "And he's not coming."

Mary nodded. "I know," she replied. "Your dad told me."

Clarissa stood up, facing Mary. "Do you hate me?" she asked, her lower lip trembling in fear.

"No, I don't hate you," Mary said, coming forward and hugging her daughter. "I don't hate you at all."

"But I made Mike go away," Clarissa sobbed. "I was mean to him and I made him go."

"Yes, you did," Mary said. "And that made me sad. Very sad. But just because you do something wrong doesn't mean I stop loving you. Love doesn't work that way. I can be disappointed and sad but still love you."

"I tried to fix it," Clarissa explained. "I tried to get him back, but he won't come."

"Did he tell you that once you sent him away, he couldn't come back?" Mary asked.

Clarissa nodded.

"Well, Mike doesn't lie," Mary said. "So, even if he wants to, he can't come back."

"But I miss him," Clarissa cried.

"I do too," Mary replied softly. "And I will miss him for a long time. But we can't change what happened. I hope, though, that you learned something from this."

"Grandma said we shouldn't say things in anger because we can't take them back," Clarissa said.

Mary put her arm around Clarissa's shoulder and guided her to the dining room table with her. She sat down and put her hands on Clarissa's shoulders. "Do you know what that means?" Mary asked.

Clarissa looked away, then met Mary's eyes and shook her head. "No," she admitted. "I don't."

"Do you remember when we were making Christmas cookies last month and your dad squeezed the frosting tube too much?" Mary asked, earning a shadow of a smile from Clarissa. "It was a mess."

Clarissa nodded.

"Do you remember what we had to do with the extra icing?" Mary asked.

"We used some of it," she said. "But most of it we had to throw away."

"Why?" Mary asked. "Why did we have to throw it away, do you remember?"

"Yes," she said. "Because once it was squeezed out we couldn't put it back inside."

"No matter how hard we tried," Mary said. "Right?"

"Right," she agreed. "It couldn't go back."

"That's what Grandma meant about saying things in anger and not being able to take them back," Mary said. "Once they're out there, we can't put them back in our mouths and unsay them."

"Like when Maggie said I was a baby?" Clarissa asked.

Mary nodded. "And what did you say to Maggie?" she asked.

"I said that machines were cooler than her and that I didn't want to be her friend," she admitted.

"How do you think that made her feel?"

Clarissa glanced down at the floor again. "Sad," she whispered, tears in her voice. "Very sad."

Mary nodded. "I think this family has had enough sad," she said. "I think you need to walk over to Maggie's and apologize. I think that's what Mike would want you to do."

Clarissa finally met Mary's eyes. "I'm so sorry you're sad," she said.

Mary smiled. "Thank you, sweetheart," she replied. "Now, go to Maggie's and get this worked out."

Chapter Sixty

On Monday morning, Mary looked out the window as Clarissa and Maggie waited for the bus together. Bradley walked up behind her, put his hands on her shoulders and leaned forward to share her view. "It's good to see them together again," he said. Then he placed a tender kiss on her neck. "Have I mentioned what a fabulous mother you are?"

She leaned back against him and sighed. "I had a really good example. Besides, Clarissa did all of the hard work. She had to swallow her pride and ask for forgiveness. That's a hard thing to do."

He slipped his hands from her shoulders, looped them around her waist and laid his head against hers. "How are you doing?" he asked softly.

Her throat tightened, and tears filled her eyes. She nodded, not trusting her voice at first. "I'm fine," she whispered. "I still, you know, miss him a lot."

Bradley nodded. "Yeah, I know," he replied. "I don't think that's going to go away for a long time."

She shook her head and brushed a few tears off her cheeks. "No, probably not," she said. "But, you know, he's probably really happy with his new person."

"Is it selfish to hope that he's as miserable as we are?" Bradley asked.

A ripple of laughter escaped her lips, and she nodded. "Probably," she said. "But it's only fair that he's as sad as we are."

The bus pulled up outside, and the girls, chatting happily with each other, climbed on together. When the bus pulled away from the curb, Mary turned in Bradley's arms to face him. "So, what's on the agenda for today?" she asked.

He looked down at her. "Well, first thing on my list is kissing my wife senseless," he said with a smile.

She looped her arms around his neck. "I can agree to that," she said. "As a matter of fact, I can move that right to the top of my list."

He smiled at her. "Good thing," he said, lowering his lips to hers and kissing her tenderly.

She sighed softly, enjoying the sweetness and the comfort of his kiss. Once the kiss ended, she put her head against his chest and absorbed the warmth of his embrace. "Can we just stay like this all day?" she asked.

He laughed softly, and she could hear the rumble through his chest. "Well, although it would be wonderful, there are a couple of problems with that," he said.

She sighed. "Name one," she asked against his chest.

"We're not close enough to a bathroom," he teased.

She sighed loudly. "Why did you have to bring that up?" she grumbled. "You just reminded my body."

She stepped out of his embrace and smiled up at him. "But I'll be back."

"I'll be here," he promised.

As she hurried up the stairs, Bradley sighed softly.

"How is she doing?" Margaret asked, walking into the living room from the kitchen.

"She's handling it," Bradley said. "And I suppose that's all any of us can do."

She nodded. "Do you think there's any chance he'll be back?"

"If there's any way possible, Mike will figure out," Bradley said.

Margaret studied him for a moment. "I realize that Mike was a special friend of Mary's," she said slowly. "But I suddenly realized that he was even more than that for you. How are you doing?"

Bradley smiled sadly. "He was like my right-hand man," he admitted with a shrug. "I kind of relied on him to watch over Mary and Clarissa when I couldn't. Suddenly, this weekend, I realized that I didn't have that backup anymore."

Margaret placed her hand on Bradley's arm. "Make sure you give yourself a chance to grieve too," she said. "You've been strong all weekend long, helping everyone else."

"Thanks, Margaret," he said. "I'll try to remember that."

She laughed softly. "I raised sons, Bradley," she said, shaking her head. "That is your polite way of saying that you really don't have time to take care of yourself right now. But you're too polite to say it out loud."

Bradley smiled at her. "You are a very wise woman," he said. "But, I really will think about what you said."

She sighed. "Thank you."

Chapter Sixty-one

Mary placed another armful of files into a cardboard box. She looked around her office space, the shelves now bare and boxes piled up in one corner. She wondered if Mike had known what was going to happen when he suggested she not renew her lease. "Why am I doing this?" she wondered aloud. "Is there a real reason here?"

With a loud sigh, she put the lid on the box and sealed it with tape. "Mike, if you can hear me," she said, "I'm so sorry it ended like this. I miss you and I love you."

The bell over her door rang, and she looked over to see Alex and Bradley walk in.

"Good morning," she said. "What's up?"

"Do you have a few minutes?" Bradley asked. "We wanted to catch up on the case."

"Sure," she replied. "I think that's a great idea."

They pulled chairs up around Mary's desk
after Bradley raided the refrigerator for bottled water
for each of them.

"Okay," Bradley said after he took his seat.
"Who's first?"

"Claeys was on the parole board," Alex said.

"What?" Mary asked. "How did that
happen?"

Shaking his head, Alex looked disgusted. "If I
were to guess, it would be that he made a
contribution to someone's political campaign," he
said. "Perfectly legal. But at this point, it would be
hard to trace it back. He was appointed just after
Carol's sentencing and stayed on the board
throughout her time."

"This is unbelievable," Mary said. "How did
this go on for so long?"

Alex shrugged. "No one looked because no
one cared," he said. "Well, except for Carol, and they
were powerful enough to silence her."

She nodded. "Well, they also silenced Dr.
Reinsband in their own way," she agreed. "They

must have been initially drugging him without his knowledge and then just continued so he would be unable to ask any questions."

"How is he doing? Bradley asked.

"Karen called me this morning and said that since he's been off those drugs he's started to regain some of his cognitive abilities."

"So, it really was the drug that kept him from being aware?" Alex asked.

"Yeah, they took an honorable doctor, one people would trust, got him to sign on to the project, and then took his health away from him," Bradley said. "So, what's our next step? Obviously, Claeys knows we're looking into this."

Mary shook her head. "But look at it from Claeys' point of view," she said. "He got to Carol Ford before we could, in his estimation. As far as he knows, Dr. Reinsband is totally useless to us. And those guys Ma heard think they got all the records."

"Who is the most dangerous?" Alex asked.

"I went to the hospital on Saturday morning and spoke with the pharmacist about the drug orders that are sent over to the prison," Bradley said. "He said the orders are generated from computer requests made by the doctors and then filled by the pharmacist at the prison. So, there doesn't need to be collusion on the pharmacist part, just a different order from the doctor."

Mary shook her head. "Aren't pharmacists supposed to know about drug interactions? Shouldn't they have caught that?"

"So, the fill-in pharmacist was one of the goons from the pharmaceutical company," Alex suggested. "If Claeys got him fake identification, it wouldn't have been an issue."

"If the autopsy shows a complication from a drug interaction caused Carol's death," Alex said, "can we trace the order back to the doctor that requested it?"

"Funny thing," Bradley said. "I had the pharmacist pull the order, and even after all of these years, Dr. Reinsband has the ability to order drugs."

"Claeys!" Mary exclaimed. "It had to be him."

Alex sat back in his chair, pondering the information they'd just shared with each other. "Okay, I can see how difficult it is having clients who can't testify in court," he finally said.

Mary smiled. "It can present its challenges," she agreed. "But it can also give us an upper hand when dealing with the bad guys."

"How?" Alex asked.

"What if one of you were to meet with Claeys?" she suggested. "And mention that you were contacted by either Ash or Hickory and they wanted to make a deal. Then ask Claeys if he's ever heard of them or dealt with them and if he thinks they would be good witnesses for the case."

Bradley smiled and nodded. "Stir things up a little," he said. "I like it. What do you think, Alex?"

"I think I need to meet with the CEO of the hospital and see what information he can share with me," he replied. He stood up and smiled at Mary. "You are brilliant. Any time you want to give up PI work and work with me, you just make a call."

"Thanks," she said with a smile. "But I think I'll stick with ghosts."

Chapter Sixty-two

Alex walked into the CEO's office and sat down in the chair across from the stylishly dressed CEO. Although, Alex reasoned as he casually unbuttoned the first button of his own Italian wool suit, the guy was not even close to his league. Leaning back and leisurely crossing his legs, Alex smiled at Dr. Claeys.

"Thank you for taking some time out of your busy day to meet with me," Alex began cordially.

Claeys smiled and nodded affably. "Well, you know, I always support the law enforcement system of our town," he said.

Alex continued to smile but had to stop himself from clenching his teeth. "Well, we all appreciate it," he was finally able to say. "And, actually, that's why I'm here. We've had a tremendous break in the case—"

Alex watched Claeys' eyes widen momentarily and then relax again. *He's good*, Alex thought.

"You did?" Claeys asked, templing his fingers as he rested his forearms on his desk. "What kind of break?"

"We received a phone call from a man who said he was a representative from the pharmaceutical company in question," Alex said. "I have his name and contact information written down in my notebook…" He patted his pocket and rolled his eyes. "Well, I guess my notebook is still on my desk." He shook his head dismissively. "Well, actually, that's not important. His name is something to do with trees, like oak or linden or…"

Claeys looked alarmed.

"Basically, to cut to the chase," Alex said, "the man said he wanted to cut a deal with my office."

"Cut a deal?" Claeys repeated, stunned.

Alex nodded again. "Yeah, people do it all the time," he replied casually. "They testify against the other people in the group for a promise of a lighter sentence. And really, considering how old this case is, I'll probably take him up on his offer."

Alex could see tiny dots of sweat forming on Claeys' forehead.

"I was just wondering if you remember any of the names of the people who were sending the hospital the monthly check." he asked. "It would be great if one of them had, you know, a tree name."

Claeys swallowed loudly and patted his forehead with his handkerchief. "Well, I can certainly go back and check," he said, and then he smiled. "So, when do you need the information?"

"The sooner the better," Alex replied. "I've got to call him back, but I'm hoping he's able to meet with me this afternoon. Tomorrow at the latest."

"Oh," Claeys replied, his voice sounding strained. "Well, good, the sooner the better."

"I totally agree," he said, standing and leaning forward to offer his hand.

Claeys' hand was warm and sweaty.

"Thanks for your help," Alex said with a smile.

"My pleasure," Claeys replied.

Turning, Alex let his smile widen. Yeah, sure it is, he thought.

Chapter Sixty-three

Mary parked her car and walked towards the doctor's office.

"Hey good-looking."

She turned and smiled at Bradley, who was hurrying towards her.

"What are you doing here?" she asked.

He didn't want to tell her that he was worried about her, worried about the sadness that had been on her face when he and Alex had arrived at her office that morning. He didn't want to even bring up Mike, knowing that it would just remind her of her loss.

"I decided to join you, if that's okay?" he finally said.

Nodding, she linked her arm through his. "That's more than okay," she replied. "That's wonderful."

They were ushered into the examination room in record time. Mary sat on the exam table while

Bradley took the patient's chair as they waited for the nurse.

"I have never gotten in here so quickly," she remarked.

Bradley shrugged. "Maybe you ought to wear a gun," he teased.

"Or bring a big, tall, handsome, gun-bearing police chief with me," she countered.

"I like that idea too," he said. "How many more of these do you have?"

"Well, next week we start on two visits a week," she said, "until Mikey's born."

"Why two visits?" he asked.

"I'm a little high-risk because of my gunshot wound and the scar tissue," she explained. "Everything seems fine, but as the time gets closer to delivery, they want to monitor me closely."

"Are you worried?" he asked.

"No," she said with a smile. Then she shrugged. "Well, a little. Mikey is strong and active, but, you know, this is my first baby."

He nodded. "And you did get kicked out of birthing class."

She grinned. "It was your fault."

"Was not."

"Was too."

"Was not what?" the nurse mid-wife asked as she walked in.

"Bradley, this is Mickey, my nurse mid-wife," Mary said. "Mickey, this is my husband, Bradley."

"Good to meet you," Mickey said. "So...was not what?"

"It was his fault we got kicked out of the birthing class," Mary replied easily.

Mickey nodded. "Yeah, we got a note about that," she said.

"Seriously?" Bradley exclaimed.

Mickey smiled. "No," she said. "But from the look on your face, I'm going to side with Mary. Your fault."

He chuckled. "It was the instructor's fault," he argued.

"The instructor?" Mickey asked.

"Hee-hee-hee-hee," Bradley demonstrated.

Laughing, Mickey nodded as she wrapped the blood pressure cuff around Mary's arm. "Okay, I can see it was her fault," she conceded. "Imagine teaching breathing techniques at a birthing class."

"I don't think I'm winning you over," Bradley said.

She inflated the cuff, placed her stethoscope on Mary's arm and then slowly deflated it. When the procedure was done she looked up at Mary. "Blood pressure's good," she said.

She sat down at the desk next to Bradley. "How's your blood pressure, daddy-to-be?" she asked as she entered Mary's information into her chart.

"I'm good," he said.

"Good," she replied. "Do you want to hear the baby's heartbeat?"

Bradley smiled. "That would be great!"

Mickey helped Mary lean back on the table and lift up her shirt to expose her belly. First, she

341

measured Mary and smiled. "You have a good-sized baby in there," she said. "You're at thirty-nine centimeters."

"Is that good?" Bradley asked.

"Yes, normally after about twenty weeks, a pregnant woman's belly will measure a centimeter for each week of pregnancy, give or take 2 centimeters," she said. "Mary's at about thirty-seven weeks, so thirty-nine centimeters is normal, but on the large size."

Picking up a white squeeze bottle, Mickey applied a generous layer of clear gel to Mary's skin. Mary jumped a little.

"Cold?" she asked.

Mary nodded. "A little."

"Sorry," she replied. "We usually keep it warm."

Mickey opened a drawer in the table and pulled out a small, handheld, ultrasonic device with a probe attached to it. She held the device in one hand and slowly moved the probe against Mary's belly. Suddenly the device emitted a rhythmic swooshing sound. Mickey turned to Bradley. "That's it," she said.

He wasn't prepared for the sudden onslaught of emotion that washed over him. Love. Wonder. Fear. Yes, definitely fear. They were going to have a baby in a few weeks' time.

Bradley stood up and walked over to Mary. "That's Mikey?" he asked, in awe, taking her hand in his.

Mary nodded and smiled at him. "Yes, that's Mikey," she replied.

Suddenly the swooshing sound was interrupted by a loud thump.

"What was that?" Bradley asked, alarmed.

"That was your son kicking me in the ribs," Mary replied. "He is such a rude child."

Bradley took a deep breath, trying to calm his pounding heart. "But he's okay, right?"

"He's more than okay," Mickey reassured him. "He's active and healthy."

She noted the heart rate on Mary's chart and then handed Mary a handful of tissue to wipe the gel from her belly. "So, any issues, any swelling, any nausea?"

Mary shook her head. "Nothing," she said. "I'm feeling great."

"You start your bi-weekly appointments next week," she reminded her. "So, the doctor will probably want to do a pelvic exam at that point."

Mary winced, and Mickey nodded. "Yeah, I totally understand," she said. "But, luckily, they don't do them as often as they used to do."

"Well, that's something," Mary said, sitting up and adjusting her shirt.

"Call me if you have any problems," Mickey said while Mary's chart and walking to the door.

"Thanks," Mary replied. "I will."

Once Mickey closed the exam room door, Bradley put his arms around Mary and hugged her. "That was amazing," he said.

She leaned against him and nodded. "Yeah, it really is," she said. "I love it every single time."

He stepped back, put his hands on her belly and bent down, placing his face against her belly.

344

"Mikey, this is your father," he said. "You need to stop kicking…"

He stopped and looked up at Mary in disbelief.

"What?" she asked.

"Your son just kicked me in the face," he replied, straightening up.

She laughed. "He must take after your side of the family," she said. "I'm sure we were never that rude."

"Yeah, right," Bradley replied, helping her off the exam table. "Just wait. I'm going to ask your mother."

Chapter Sixty-four

"She not only kicked me," Margaret said that evening at dinner. "She insisted on coming two weeks late."

Bradley looked at Margaret and shook his head sympathetically. Then he turned and sent Mary a triumphant smile. "I don't even need to say I told you so," he said.

"You just said I told you so," Mary replied evenly. "You can't say you don't need to say it and then say it. It doesn't work that way."

Bradley shook his head. "What did you just say?" he asked.

"And just think," Margaret inserted. "If we're lucky, you'll have two people in your family who think like that. Mikey will be just like his mom."

Bradley's smile disappeared, and Mary chuckled softly.

"I never thought of that," he said. "Two O'Reillys."

"Aye," Margaret said. "They'll certainly keep you on your toes."

Clarissa looked from Margaret to Bradley. "But I thought Mikey would be an Alden," she said.

Mary leaned over and put her arm around her daughter's shoulders. "Oh, he will, sweetheart," she said. "We're just teasing."

"Oh," Clarissa replied. "Well, I think Mikey should be like Mommy, because I'm like Daddy. So, it will be two and two."

"Exactly," Mary said. "Two and two."

Bradley shook his head. "I can hardly wait," he said with apprehension. Then he turned to Clarissa. "But you'll be on my side, right?"

Clarissa giggled. "Right," she said. "Except for when I'm on Mom's side."

"That sounds about right," Margaret said.

Mary stood up and started clearing the table. "So, what kind of homework do you have tonight?" she asked Clarissa.

"Only some reading," Clarissa replied. "It's easy."

"Good," Bradley said. "Because I forgot to tell your mom that we have an appointment tonight."

"We do?" Mary asked. "Where?"

Bradley stood and picked up the dinner plates. "Mel called me and said that it would be easier for him to turn the power off on the third-floor wing in the evening. No one from administration would be there to monitor it."

"That makes sense," she said. "Ma, would you..."

"I would love to read with Clarissa," she said. "And, as a matter of fact, I was going to ask you two to go out anyway."

"Oh, what for?" Mary asked, coming over to clear the serving bowls.

"Well, it looks like we're in for quite a storm by the end of the week," Margaret said. "And I thought we should stock up on some supplies."

"Like soup and bread?" Bradley asked.

Mary and Margaret looked at each other and laughed. "Oh, Bradley," Mary said. "Not soup and bread. Hot chocolate, marshmallows and the ingredients for oatmeal cookies."

"How silly of me," Bradley replied. "But can we also throw in ingredients for chili and chocolate chip cookies?"

"Now you're talking," Margaret said.

"Okay, after the hospital, we'll run by the store," Mary said. "Thanks, Ma."

Chapter Sixty-five

The elevator stopped on the third floor, and Bradley looked down at his phone. "There is absolutely no service here in the elevator," he said. "I'll text Mel once we're on the floor."

The doors opened, and they stepped out into the lobby. Bradley looked down at his phone. "Bars. Finally."

He texted their location to Mel and received a reply. "Okay, flashlights on," he said. "Mel said we've got thirty seconds."

They walked past the nurses station, through the double doors and down the dim corridor towards the hidden unit. Suddenly, the emergency lights turned off, and they were plunged into blackness except for the beams from their flashlights.

"Okay, we've got twenty minutes," Bradley said. "Let's hope Jack is willing to let us in again."

They hurried down to the end of the hall. Bradley had the keys Maggie had found, just in case

Jack wasn't on duty. They were only steps from the door when it slowly creaked open on its own.

"Thanks, Jack," Mary said. She grabbed hold of Bradley's hand so they both could see the little boy holding the door open, his back pressed against the wooden door.

"The bad men came here," Jack said. "They came to the room."

"Yeah, we heard about that," Bradley said.

"Carol is here," Jack said. "She's here to take care of us."

"Carol's here?" Mary exclaimed, flashing her light down the narrow hallway.

The woman suddenly appeared right next to her, and Mary jumped.

Carol laughed. "Sorry about that," she said. "I'm just getting used to this."

Mary exhaled slowly. "That's okay," she said. "I'm just glad you're here with the children."

"They have always been my kids," Carol said. "I'm glad to be reunited with them."

"We wanted to come back here before they demolished the unit," Bradley said. "And make sure we got any final evidence cleared out."

Jack looked from Bradley to Carol and shook his head. "Carol, are they your friends?"

"Yes, Jack, they are," she replied. "And they're your friends too."

Jack looked up at Bradley and smiled. "You look like my dad," he said. "He was a soldier."

"Wow. Soldiers are very special people," Bradley replied, squatting down to be on Jack's level. "I bet you were pretty proud of him."

Jack nodded excitedly. "Yeah. I was," he said. "Hey, do you want to see where we sleep?"

"Where you sleep?" Bradley asked.

"Uh, huh!" Jack said, gliding down the hall. "Come on!"

They followed Jack past the small nurses station and continued past all of the tiny hospital rooms. "Jack, where are you…" Bradley paused when Jack stopped in front of a solid wood door at the far end of the hallway. "What is this?"

"It's where we all sleep," Jack said, and then he disappeared through the door.

The door started to slowly open. Holding tightly to each other's hands, Mary and Bradley entered the room together. Mary's flashlight was the first to shine onto the row of small, metal doors built into the wall.

"Oh, no," she cried, turning her face into Bradley's arm.

"Jack," Bradley called, his voice tight with emotion. "Are you still in here?"

Jack appeared next to him. "I'm here," he said with a wide smile.

"Do all of the baker's dozen sleep in here?" he asked.

Jack nodded. "Yeah, when we were done in our rooms, they moved us in here," he replied.

"Are you sure someone didn't move you anywhere else?" he asked.

Jack shook his head. "No, they just moved us in here and locked the doors."

Bradley pulled his phone out of his pocket and looked down. One bar. He was going to try it. He pressed a number. "Alex," he said when the phone was answered, "I need you to get down to the hospital right away. The third-floor unit." He took a deep breath before he could continue. "There's a morgue at the end of the hall, and I think all of the children's bodies are still here."

Chapter Sixty-six

Mary sat just outside the yellow, crime scene tape that was now stretched from the nurses station to the elevator wall. She watched as the forensic photographers and evidence collectors came up on the elevator, ducked under the tape and hurried down through the double doors. Then she watched as thirteen gurneys carrying black, zippered bags were rolled past her.

A few minutes later, Bradley and Alex came out from behind the double doors. "We're almost done," Bradley said.

"I can't believe they were going to demolish this unit with those bodies still in there," Alex said, his voice teeming with disgust.

"Yeah, it doesn't make any sense to me either," Mary said.

Alex looked over and shook his head. "Oh, no, I know why they tried to do it," he said. "My friend in Bloomington, Nick Butzirus, called me this afternoon. The medications they were giving the kids were destroying their livers. Not only was it unauthorized, but the level was lethal, especially for children. They kept those bodies in there so no one could perform an autopsy and figure out what they'd done."

"So, we're not talking just negligence any longer," Bradley said. "We're talking murder."

Alex nodded. "The kids may have been sick, but those drugs speeded up the process and gave them months of torturous pain."

"So, even if we can't get them for Carol's death…" Mary began.

"We can get them for this," Alex said. "I've called the judge for a warrant for Claeys, Ash and Hickory."

"As soon as you've got it, I'll send some cars out to round them up," Bradley said.

A final police officer came out from behind the double doors. "Everything's closed up," he told Bradley.

"Thank you," Bradley said. "I'll see you tomorrow."

"Are we done?" Alex said.

"Yeah, we can go," Bradley said, ducking under the crime tape.

Mary placed a hand on his chest to stop him. "No, we can't," she said.

He stopped and looked at her. "Why not?"

"Because I need to go see the kids," she said. "With their bodies gone, they might be ready to go to the light."

Alex held up the crime tape. "After you, Mrs. Alden," he said.

"Oh, Alex, you don't have to stay," she said.

"Are you kidding?" he asked. "I don't want to miss this."

The emergency lights were on in the hallway, and the door to the unit was propped open. Mary walked to the doorway. "Carol, are you here?" she asked.

Carol appeared next to her. "I've been with the kids," she said. "They've been pretty upset with so much activity."

"I can imagine," Mary said. "But the men responsible will be prosecuted for their crimes, and these kids can finally rest in peace."

"Well, praise the Lord," Carol replied.

"I need you to call them so we can help them move on," Mary requested.

Carol nodded and turned to face the long hallway. "Kids, come on out now," she called. "It's safe, and Mary, the nice lady who is my friend, is here to help you again."

Bradley grabbed Alex's arm, guiding his hand to Mary's shoulder. Then he took Mary's hand. They could all see thirteen little ghosts slowly come out from various doorways and travel hesitantly towards them.

"Hi, kids," Mary said softly.

They smiled shyly.

"I'm so sorry this happened to you," she said. "I'm so sorry there was no one here to protect you and watch over you."

They nodded wordlessly.

"I want you to know that Carol tried to help you," Mary explained. "But the bad guys locked her up so she couldn't get to you."

Their eyes widened, and they turned to look at Carol. "I'm so sorry, babies," she said.

"But now," Mary continued, "you get to go to a place where you will never be afraid or sad again. A place where your families are waiting for you. A place of light and warmth and love."

"There's no such place," Anna said, shaking her head.

"Yes, there is," Mary said. "I promise. And it's so close by. All you have to do is look around and you'll see—"

"The light!" Jack screamed in terror. "The light is coming! Run!"

"Wait!" Mary cried. "The light is good."

"No, it's not!" Anna cried. "The doctor used the light. They would shine it in our faces so we couldn't see what they were doing to us. The light hurt us."

"But this light is different," Mary insisted. "This light is a good light."

Jack shook his head. "I hate doctors," he said. "And I hate lights."

Then he faded away, along with all the other children.

Mary looked at Bradley. "What are we going to do?" she asked.

"Whatever it is, we have to do it quickly," he said. "They could still demolish this place on Friday."

Chapter Sixty-seven

The bus pulled up in front of the house on Thursday morning as Mary, Bradley and Margaret watched from the window.

"I can't believe they didn't close school," Margaret said as they walked back to the kitchen. "They're calling for blizzard conditions."

"But not until this evening," Bradley said. "So, she should be home from school well before it hits."

"When will you be home?" Mary asked Bradley, sipping from her cup of tea.

He shrugged into his jacket. "It all depends on how bad the storm is," he said. "I might be out all night."

"Well, just be careful out there," she said.

"Are you staying home today?" Margaret asked Mary.

"I can't, even though I want to," she replied. "I was at the hospital all day yesterday, trying to

361

convince the kids that the light wasn't scary, but they wouldn't listen to me. So, I have one more idea."

"What's that?" Bradley asked.

"I'm going to go to the nursing home and see if Karen feels that Dr. Reinsband is up to traveling," she said. "The kids knew him. He was their nice doctor. Maybe he can convince them."

"I sure hope that works," Bradley said. "Just be careful and get home early."

She nodded. "I plan on getting home way before the first snowflake drops from the sky."

Margaret hugged herself and shivered slightly.

"Ma, are you okay?" Mary asked.

"I'm feeling a little anxious about the day," she answered. "Maybe it's just the drop in barometric pressure. But I'll feel much better when all of you are home safe with a cup of cocoa in your hands and a fire blazing in the fireplace."

Mary leaned over and kissed her mother on the cheek. "Well, don't worry too much," she said.

"We'll have a fun snow day tomorrow, and bonus, it's Friday the 13th. So we can have double the fun."

"Isn't Friday the 13th supposed to be unlucky?" Bradley asked.

Mary shook her head. "Not if you're an O'Reilly," she said. "Then it's one of the luckiest days of the year."

Bradley shook his head. "Well good, we could use a little luck," he said. He gave a quick kiss goodbye. "I'll call you."

"Okay," she said. "Remember, be safe!"

Chapter Sixty-eight

A few hours later, Mary was sitting in the same room at the nursing home she and Bradley had sat in a week earlier. But this time, Karen was assisting her with her meeting with Dr. Reinsband.

"Last week I asked you to consider going back to the hospital," Mary said. "And today I'm here to ask you to please consider it again."

Dr. Reinsband shook his head. "I'm so sorry," he said sadly. "But, right now, the idea of going back to that hospital— after understanding what happened to me because of that hospital— I just can't. They stole my life. They stole my whole life."

"It wasn't the hospital, Dr. Reinsband, that did this to you," Mary countered. "It was a few very greedy, very bad men. And, the children are as much victims as you were. More so, because they never had a choice. They never got a payout. They were human guinea pigs."

"What do you want me to say?" he yelled. "I was wrong. I neglected them. I helped to cause their pain."

"No," she said. "Because all of that is about you and your guilt. What I want you to do, no, what those kids need you to do is go back to the hospital and apologize. Help them understand that that light, that eternal light that is so important, is not something to be afraid of."

He shook his head. "I can't do it," he said softly, not meeting Mary's eyes. "I just can't do it."

Mary stood up, frustrated and angry. "No, that's not true," she said. "You are choosing not to do it. You are choosing to let those children suffer again. You are choosing to let them become scattered souls because you are too afraid." She exhaled heavily. "Well, I hope you can live with yourself."

She turned and marched out of the room.

"Mary," Karen called, running down the hall after her. "Mary, are you okay?"

Mary nodded, trying to hold her tears back. "I'm sorry, Karen," she said. "I shouldn't have lost my temper like that—"

Karen shook her head. "No, you had every right to say what you did," she said. "I'll call you if he changes his mind."

Mary nodded. "Thanks," she said, and then she winced.

"Are you okay?" Karen asked, concerned.

"I must have gotten up too quickly in there," Mary said. "My lower back is aching. But it's no big deal. I'll go back to my office and put a heating pad on it."

"An ice pack," Karen advised. "That's better for it."

"Thanks," Mary said, smiling at her friend. "An ice pack it is."

She worked through the rest of the day, replacing ice packs and massaging her lower back as she looked through files. But the pile of files didn't get any smaller because she couldn't concentrate on anything. Finally, she pulled out her phone and called Alex.

"Is there any way was can stop demolition from happening tomorrow?" she asked him.

"I wish there was, Mary," Alex replied. "But since I can't tell them the real reason why, I don't have a good enough excuse to stop it."

"Could we just lie?" she asked.

He chuckled softly. "If I could think up a good enough lie, I would do that too," he said. "But I've got nothing. I'm sorry."

She sighed. "That's okay," she said. "I was just looking for a miracle."

"Keep looking, Mary," he said. "Don't give up on miracles yet."

She hung up and looked at the clock on the wall. It was almost four-thirty, and the sky was already starting to darken. Maybe she would just call it a day and head home.

She had just stood up to get her coat when her phone rang. She reached for it and saw that it was Karen. "Hi, Karen. What's up?" she asked.

"Dr. Reinsband is willing to try to talk to the children," she said. "We can meet you at the hospital in a half-hour. Does that work?"

"Oh, Karen, that would be so wonderful," Mary replied. "Yes, I'll meet you there."

She hung up with Karen and called her mother. "Hi, Ma," she said. "I just got a call from Karen at the nursing home. Dr. Reinsband just agreed to try to talk to the children. They want me to meet them at the hospital at five. So, don't worry. I'm going to be a little later than I thought."

"Mary, the storm is supposed to be fierce," Margaret said. "I don't like the idea of you traveling in it."

"If it looks like it's too bad by the time I'm done," Mary said, "I'll head up to the fourth floor and hang out with Rosie and Stanley until Bradley can come and drive me home. How does that sound?"

Mary could hear her mother's sigh of relief. "That sounds like a perfect plan," she said. "Okay, be careful, and good luck with the children."

"Thank you, Ma," she said. "Have a safe night with Clarissa."

Chapter Sixty-nine

Big, fat snowflakes dropped down onto her windshield as Mary drove from her office downtown to the hospital. The ache in her back hadn't subsided, but she was almost getting used to it. She parked near the emergency room and hurried down the hallway to the elevator.

"Hey, Mary. Mary O'Reilly."

She turned to see a man dressed in a maintenance uniform jogging her way. "Mel?" she asked.

He smiled. "I was hoping I'd see you," he said. "It was great what you guys did upstairs. Just great."

She smiled at him. "Well, we couldn't have done it without your help," she replied. "Thank you so much."

He shrugged, a little embarrassed. "So, what are you doing here now?" he asked. "The storm is supposed to be a big one."

"Yeah, I know," she said. "But Dr. Reinsband is coming by in a little while to meet me on the third floor to make sure that we've gotten everything we need for the case. I shouldn't be up there too long."

"Okay, well, you just holler if you need anything," he said. "I'll be here all night."

"Thanks, Mel. Thanks a lot."

She hurried to the elevator and pressed the button for three. The elevator arrived quickly and went directly up to the third floor. Mary stepped off the elevator and rubbed her back again. "I must have really pulled something," she murmured, using the base of her hand to push against her lower back.

An hour and a half later the elevator opened again, and Karen and Dr. Reinsband stepped out. "I'm so sorry," Karen apologized. "With storm preparations at the nursing home, I got delayed."

"That's okay," Mary said, getting up from the folding chair she'd found in the supply room. "What's important is that you're here now."

"Wow, this brings back memories," he said. "I spent so many hours in these halls."

"Thank you for coming," Mary said.

He turned and took her hands in his. "Thank you for being bold enough to tell me the truth," he said. "You were right. I need to try and help these kids."

Mary led the way through the double doors and to the end of the hallway. The door to the unit was still propped open, so they all stepped inside.

"Where should we go?" Dr. Reinsband asked.

Carol appeared next to Mary, glancing at Dr. Reinsband. "Well, you performed a miracle," she said. "The children are at the end of the hall in the old television room."

"They're in the television room," Mary said.

"And you know that because?" he asked.

"Carol Ford, their social worker, just told me," Mary replied bluntly. "She was killed by Claeys last week."

"Oh, I am so sorry to hear that," Dr. Reinsband said. "Carol was a good, good woman."

Mary nodded. "Yes, she was," she said.

"I still am," Carol said. "Just because I'm dead doesn't mean I'm going to change my ways."

Mary laughed. "That's true," she replied.

"What's true?" Karen asked.

"Carol said that she's still a good woman," Mary answered. "Now, let's hurry down to the television room and see what we can do."

Mary walked in first. The television room now consisted of old, gray carpet, empty spaces on the floor where furniture used to stand, rusted hardware on the wall for hanging a television, and a light fixture hanging drunkenly from the ceiling.

"This is not how I remember this room," the doctor said. He shook his head and walked into the room behind her.

Mary saw all of the children look up in surprise when he entered the room.

"The children are here," she said. "And they can see you."

He nodded and then shook his head. "I'm here to tell you how sorry I am," he said. "You put your trust in me, and I betrayed that trust. I should have never trusted those other men with you. They told me that you were getting better. They told me that the medicine was working. They told me that you were happy. They lied to me. But I should have checked on you."

"Why didn't you check on us?" Jack asked.

"Jack asked why you didn't check on them," Mary repeated.

"Well, soon after I agreed to work with those men, I started getting sick," he explained. "I couldn't think clearly. I couldn't remember things. And I stopped taking care of people."

"Did you get better?" Jack asked.

"Jack wants to know if you got better," Mary said.

"Last week, this nice lady and her husband came to the place where I live," he said. "They talked to my doctors and they found out that the medicine I'd been given was hurting me, causing me to not think clearly."

"The medicine hurt us too," Anna said.

"Anna said the medicine hurt them too."

"I know," he replied. "Mary told me what happened to you. I almost didn't come because I was afraid."

"Afraid of what?" Anna asked, confused.

Without needing to hear Anna's comment, Dr. Reinsband continued. "I was afraid you would hate me forever for not being here when you needed me," he said. "I was afraid you would think that I wanted this to happen to you. I was afraid that you would be afraid of me too. And that would break my heart."

"What about the light?" Jack asked.

"Jack wants to know about the light," Mary said and prayed silently that Dr. Reinsband would say the right thing.

"Well, I want you to know that those bad men who hurt you are in jail," he said. "The police picked them up yesterday. And so, they can't hurt you anymore. The light they used was broken a long time ago. So, there is no bad light. The only light that you've been seeing lately, the one that Carol and Mary showed you, that's a good light. But, it's not really a light. It's a passageway. It's like when you're going down a slide with a tunnel and it's dark, but you can see the light on the other side. That's what you're seeing. It's the end of the tunnel. It's the end of being scared. It's the end of being sad. It's heaven."

Chapter Seventy

"Can you see the light?" Mary asked the children. "Look around you. Can you see it?"

Jack nodded. "I can see it," he said. "But I'm still scared."

"I can see it too," Carol said. "And it's a glorious sight to behold."

She turned to look at the children. "Why don't we all go together?" she asked. "We can all hold hands."

Jack glided over to Carol and tucked his hand securely inside hers. "I'll go with you, Carol," he said. "I'm the gatekeeper, so I should be at the front of the line."

Anna sighed but then came over and held onto Jack's hand. "I'm the oldest," she said. "I'll go next. I'm not afraid."

Once Anna had stepped forward, the other eleven children slowly moved forward and took their place in line. Carol smiled down on her little chain of children. "Are we all ready to go?" she asked them.

When they all nodded their assent, Carol turned to Mary. "God bless you for all you have done," she said. "These children will find peace because of you."

Mary smiled, tears filling her eyes. "Thank you for loving these children and bringing them home."

"What's happening?" Karen whispered.

"Carol is taking the children to the light," Mary said. "They are all hand in hand walking together. It's perfect."

Suddenly, the dingy room was filled with golden light that slowly dimmed as each spirit walked beyond Mary's sight. The room was nearly back to normal when Mary heard Jack call out, "Look, it's my dad. He's waving to me."

With a shuddering sigh, she turned to Karen and Dr. Reinsband. "They're all gone," she said. "They made it back home. Thank you."

"That was beautiful," Dr. Reinsband said. "I could feel the warmth and the love."

Mary nodded. "It really is a wonderful thing to experience," she agreed. She turned to Karen, who was wiping her eyes with a tissue. "Thank you again."

Karen stepped up and hugged Mary. "No, thank you," she said. "I'm so glad we got here in time."

Then Karen looked down at her watch. "Oh, my," she said. "This took longer than I thought. It's nearly eight. I'd better get Dr. Reinsband back to the nursing home."

"The storm is probably going strong," Mary said. "Are you sure you want to drive?"

"Oh, we're only a few blocks away," she said. "I'm sure the plows are already out there. How about you?"

"Well, I'm first going to make a stop at the ladies room," she whispered to Karen. "Then I think I'll take the elevator up to the fourth floor and hang out with a friend of mine who's up there until Bradley gets off work."

"That's a good idea," Karen said. "I wasn't feeling good about you driving home."

"Yeah, me too," Mary said. "And my back is aching, so it will be nice to just relax for a little while."

"Let's go, doctor," Karen said. "We've got to face a winter wonderland together."

All three walked down the hall together until they reached the ladies room. "This is my stop," Mary said. "I'll talk to you soon."

Mary was relieved that the lights worked, and just to be sure, she checked her stall for toilet paper before she sat down. A few minutes later, she was feeling much better as she pressed the up button for the elevator. Mary waited for a few minutes, but the elevator finally arrived and the doors slid open.

Stepping inside, she pressed the button for the fourth floor and relaxed against the elevator wall, trying to relieve some of the pressure on her back. The elevator doors closed, and the elevator started to ascend. But, suddenly, it jerked to a stop, and the lights inside went out.

"This is so not funny," Mary said, searching in her purse for the flashlight. She found it, turned it on and shone it on the panel to find the emergency phone. She lifted the phone, but there was no tone. She clicked on the receiver, but it didn't make a difference. She studied the panel to see if there was an emergency button but could only find a "stop" button.

"Well, I don't need one of those," she grumbled. She pulled out her phone and called Bradley. She waited, with the phone to her ear, but nothing happened.

She closed her eyes in frustration. "That's right. There's no service in this elevator," she moaned. "Okay, think Mary. It's probably a power outage caused by the storm. The emergency generators will kick in in about ten minutes tops. So, all I have to do is wait for ten minutes. No big deal. What's the worst that can happen?"

Suddenly, Mary felt a rush of water run down her legs. "I just went to the bathroom," she complained. Then her jaw dropped, and her stomach clenched. "Oh, crap, I think my water just broke."

Chapter Seventy-one

Margaret paced to the window one more time. She looked out at the snow piling up on the porch, steps and street. In the few hours since it started, they must have gotten eight inches of snow. She was certainly glad that Mary had decided to stay at the hospital with Stanley and Rosie. The phone rang, and she hurried to answer it. "Aldens," she answered.

"Hi, Margaret," Bradley's voice came through the receiver. "It's Bradley. I need to speak with Mary."

"Oh, she's not here," Margaret said. "I thought she would have called you."

"What?" Bradley asked. "Where is she?"

Margaret's heart began to pound. "She had to meet Karen and Dr. Reinsband at the hospital at five. She said if the snow was too bad when she was done, she would go up to Stanley's room and visit with them until you could pick her up and drive her home."

"She hasn't called me yet," Bradley said. He looked down at the digital clock in his cruiser. It was nine-thirty. "I'm going to call Stanley's room."

"Thank you," Margaret said. "And could you call me back and let me know what's happening?"

"Of course," Bradley replied, "as soon as I know." He looked out the window at the jack-knifed semi on Highway 75 just before the bypass. The semi was blocking both lanes of traffic, and visibility was near zero. He got out of his cruiser and walked over to one of his officers at the scene. "I've got to take another call," he said. "Are you okay?"

The officer nodded. "Yeah, we got flares on both sides, and the wrecker said they'd be here in twenty minutes," he said. "I'm good."

"Thanks," Bradley replied and hurried back to his cruiser. He put it into four-wheel-drive and turned the cruiser back towards town. He pressed his radio. "Hey, this is Alden," he said to the dispatcher. "Can you patch me into the hospital switchboard?"

He waited another few moments for the hospital to answer. "Hi. I'd like Stanley Wagner's room please," he asked.

He was put on hold again as they connected him to Stanley.

The big snowflakes were flying so rapidly against his windshield he felt like he was in a science fiction movie and had just gone into warp drive. His cruiser was handling pretty well in the deep snow, but he was taking things slowly so he didn't end up in a ditch.

"Hello?" Stanley's voice echoed through the inside of the car.

"Hi, Stanley. It's Bradley."

"Snowy enough for ya?"

"Yeah, it is," Bradley responded, trying to keep the fear out of his voice. "Hey, is Mary there?"

"No, she's not." Stanley's voice was not teasing anymore. "Why would you think she is?"

"Because she told Margaret that if she was delayed at the hospital, she'd go up and visit with you and Rosie."

"She ain't here," Stanley said. "What do you want me to do?"

Panic gripped Bradley's heart. "Nothing," he said. "I'm sure it was just a miscommunication."

"You ain't thinking nothing of the kind," Stanley remarked. "But you do what you gotta do, and you call me iffen you need anything."

"Thank you, Stanley," Bradley said. He hung up the phone and started to call for Mike when he remembered that Mike was gone.

"Dammit. Dammit. Dammit," he slammed his fist against his steering wheel. "Mary! Where the hell are you?"

Chapter Seventy-two

Mary sat in the corner of the elevator, her feet stretched out in front of her and her hands rubbing her belly. "It's okay, Mikey," she breathed. "There's no need to worry. Someone's bound to realize we're missing."

Another contraction hit, and she winced, pushing against the walls to deal with the pain. Once the contraction passed, she took a slow, cleansing breath, remembering that from the video, and inhaled deeply. "How am I supposed to do this?" she wondered aloud. "I can't have a baby in an elevator."

She shivered and tried to wrap her coat closer around her body. The elevator shaft had no heat going through it, and her pants were soaked from her water breaking. She wanted to cry. She wanted to throw her no-bars phone against the wall. She wanted to scream with rage. But, there was a tiny baby inside of her who was trying to be born, so she needed to stay calm, needed to stay sane. "I need a plan," she said. "I need to come up with a plan."

She pointed her flashlight up to the roof of the elevator and saw that there was a hatch up there. "So, all I need to do is shimmy up the side of the walls, climb through a fairly small hatchway and then hoist myself up onto the top of the elevator," she murmured. "Then I can either somehow climb up to the next floor, jimmy open the doors and slide through the opening or end up giving birth on the top of an elevator."

She turned her flashlight off. "We are officially discarding the escape hatch plan."

She reached over and picked up her phone, checking it once again to see if the bars had changed. Sighing, she shook her head. "We are also officially discarding the miraculous appearance of bars plan."

She rubbed her belly again. "Don't worry, Mikey," she said. "I'll come up with another plan."

Another contraction hit, and she groaned with the pressure. She dug her nails into the material on the walls of the elevator and held on. Panting heavily, she bit her lip as the pain washed over her. Finally, the contraction subsided, and she gasped for breath. "Those are coming a little bit closer together," she breathed. "You might want to try and slow things down a little, Mikey."

She leaned her head back against the wall, tears slipping from her eyes onto her cheeks. "God, I'm really frightened," she prayed. "Don't tell Mikey, but I'm really, really scared. If there's a way you could get me out of here or send someone to help, that would be so great. Or put bars on my phone." A sob escaped her lips. "I just…I just don't want my baby to die. Please. Please help me."

Chapter Seventy-three

"Mel!" Bradley exclaimed through the phone. "Have you seen Mary?"

"Yeah, I saw her earlier this evening," he said. "She was going up to three to meet with some folks."

"Did you see her leave?" Bradley asked.

"No, I didn't," he said. "But when she was walking in, she was coming from the emergency room entrance. I'm near there right now. What kind of car does she have?"

Bradley described Mary's SUV.

"Yeah, it's still here," Mel said. "She's not with her friends on four?"

'No. I just called them, and she never made it up there," Bradley replied.

"Well, she's either on three or on four," he said. "I'll go up to three and see if I can find her."

"Thank you," Bradley said. "I'm on my way there. I should be there in a few minutes."

"I'll call you when I get up to three," Mel replied. "I know I'd lose the connection in the elevator."

Bradley hung up his phone and increased his speed, his knuckles white as he held the steering wheel tightly, maneuvering through the snow drifts. He was driving down Stephenson and was coming up to Galena when he saw a car sliding through the intersection. He applied pressure to his brakes, but the cruiser slid forward. He pulled the steering wheel to the left, missing the car in the intersection, and then whipped it to the right, praying that he was on snow and not ice and the car would stay on the road. The tires were on solid ground and responded. Bradley swung forward and continued down Stephenson Street towards the hospital.

The rest of the drive was deserted, and he nearly spun out when he turned into the hospital parking lot. He pulled up and parked next to Mary's car, then jumped out and ran to the entrance of the hospital. He'd just gone through the sliding doors when his phone rang.

"I'm up on three," Mel said immediately. "And I just discovered the second elevator is stuck between three and four."

"That's it," Bradley called. "Any other place, she would have called. She must be in the elevator. I'm on my way up to four."

"Okay, you come up," Mel said. "I'm gonna get some rope and a harness. I'm figuring you want to be the guy that gets lowered down."

"Yes," Bradley said. "I do."

He didn't trust the elevator, so he ran up the stairs three at a time. He burst onto the fourth floor and rushed to the elevator banks. Mel came running up behind him with a long crow bar in his hands. "I figured we could use this to pry it open," he said.

They angled the bar into the seam between the two doors and pushed. The door slowly opened several inches. They continued to push, one on each side, until they were fully open and exposing the elevator shaft. Mel handed Bradley a piece of wood to wedge between the doors. "It'll hold them open," he said. "I use it when I do repairs."

With the doors wedged open, Bradley leaned over and looked down. The elevator was about six feet below the fourth floor. "Mary," he called down. "Mary!"

"Bradley?"

"Are you okay?" he called, his voice shaking with relief.

"I'm in labor," she called back. "Mikey's…"

He heard her cry of pain. "Mary," he called. "I'm coming!"

He looked at the nurses who had been watching everything. "I need an emergency labor and delivery kit," he said. "And I need some blankets and some water."

He turned to Mel. "After you lower me down," he said, "can you see about getting this elevator moving? I'd rather have her give birth in a bed."

Mel nodded and handed him an LED lantern. "It's going to be dark in the elevator," he said. "And just in case you end up delivering a baby, you're going to want to see what's going on."

Bradley wrapped the rope around his waist and reached over for the steel ladder that ran along the inside of the shaft. He carefully made his way down until he was at the same height as the elevator. The elevator box was about two feet from the wall. He reached one hand over and grabbed hold of a cable, then pulled himself onto the top of the box.

"Bradley?" Mary called from inside.

"Almost there, sweetheart," he called back.

Finding the latch for the hatch, he unlocked it and pulled it off of the opening, setting it to the side. He knelt down, turned on the lantern and looked inside. Mary was sitting in the corner, her face pale and contorted in pain. She finally exhaled slowly, opened her eyes and saw him looking down at her.

"Hey," she whimpered softly.

"Hey yourself," he replied. "Want a little company?"

"Sure," she said, sniffing back a tear.

He lowered himself down into the center of the box, placed the lantern on the floor and knelt down beside his wife.

"Bradley, I'm so glad you're here," she cried.

He wrapped his arms around her and held her tightly. "I am too, sweetheart," he said. "I am too."

Chapter Seventy-four

Bradley held her hands during the next two contractions, encouraging her all the way through them. "You're doing great," he said. "Just a little bit longer."

She leaned against him, gasping for air, once the contraction ceased. "This is not how I pictured it," she breathed.

Mel sent down the labor and delivery kit and a bag of blankets. Bradley pulled out the first blanket and wrapped it around Mary's shoulders.

"Oh, it's warm," she said gratefully. "I've been so cold."

He unfolded the plastic tarp in the kit and laid it on the floor. "Come on, sweetheart," he said. "Let's get you off the wet floor and on this, okay? It's much more sanitary."

She started to move, and another contraction hit. She cried out, and Bradley pulled her into his arms and held her while her body reacted to the pressure. Finally, he could feel her relaxing, so he pushed the tarp back against the wall of the elevator and placed her on it.

"Okay, now we have a lovely hospital gown," he said.

"But, I'm so cold," she protested.

"You can keep everything from the waist up on, as long as it's not wet," Bradley said.

She nodded. "Okay, deal."

He helped her pull off her wet jeans and her underwear and put them to the side. He slipped the hospital gown on over her shirt and sweater, and then he placed the remaining warm blankets on top of her. "You look adorable," he said, placing a kiss on her nose and kneeling down next to her.

"Thanks," she said, and she had to admit she was feeling better.

She took a deep breath. "I'm beginning to feel nauseous," she said. "That's a sign of transition."

"You know what that means, don't you?" he asked. "Hee. Hee. Hee."

A chuckle burst from her lips, and she leaned against him. "That's not fair," she said. "You can't make me laugh when I'm in labor."

"Actually, I just want you to relax," he said. "As much as you can when you're giving birth in an elevator."

She chuckled again. "Okay, I'll relax," she teased. "After the baby is born."

She moaned and turned towards him. Bradley put his arm around her and slowly rubbed her back. "You're doing great," he whispered. "Keep it up. Only a little bit longer."

He felt himself tense up as she tensed up and only finally relaxed when she relaxed.

"Did Mel think he could fix the elevator?" she asked.

"He was going to try to do it as quickly as he could," he replied.

"It's not fast enough," Mary said.

"Why?" Bradley asked.

She turned to him, her eyes filled with concern. "Because I want to push."

Chapter Seventy-five

"Push," Bradley repeated, trying to sound more optimistic than he felt. "Yeah, okay, we can do this."

"Mary!" a woman's voice called from above them. "This is Mickey. How are you doing?"

"She wants to push," Bradley yelled back, looking up at the hatch.

"How far apart between contractions?" Mickey called back down.

He turned back to see that Mary's eyes were closed and her breathing shallow. "She's having one now," he called. "And they are coming every couple of minutes."

"Well, she could be ready to push," the nurse mid-wife called back. "Have you checked to see if she's crowning?"

"What? No," Bradley replied.

He looked at Mary, who looked tired but was no longer having a contraction. "Crowning?" he asked.

"You need to check to see if the baby's head is visible," she replied, panting slowly.

"Okay, Mel says that it's not safe to have one more person in there until we know what's going on," Mickey called. "So, I can trade places…"

A look of panic entered Mary's eyes.

"I'm not leaving," Bradley called up. "But, I'm a cop. I've done this lots of times."

"How many times?" Mary asked.

He smiled at her and shrugged. "Um, lots."

A ghost of a smile played on her lips. "Um, never?" she asked.

"My cat had kittens once," he whispered back.

"Okay, during the next contraction, check to see if the baby's head is visible," Mickey called down.

Bradley took his jacket off and put it behind Mary to support her back. Then he sat down in front of her, with her feet on his shoulders. He looked at her and winked. "I'm so glad we're not taking videos of this birth."

She laughed and then groaned as another contraction hit. Bradley watched in amazement as he could see the very top of the baby's head appear. He looked up at her, his eyes glistening with tears. "I can see him," he whispered. "I can see Mikey."

She smiled back. "Really? He's really there?"

"The baby is crowning," he called up, his voice thick with emotion.

"Okay, Mary," Mickey called back. "You can push with this next contraction, but don't be too crazy. We want a slow exit, not a launch."

Mary leaned back against Bradley's coat and nodded.

"She's got that," Bradley called.

"And Bradley, your job is to catch and guide," Mickey said. "No pulling or tugging allowed at all."

"Got it!"

"Do you have the kit next to you?" Mickey asked.

"Yeah," he said. "It's right here."

"Make sure the bulb syringe is close by, but you might be able to clear the baby's nose and mouth with your hand," she called. "And have a towel close by, because he's gonna be slippery."

Bradley placed a towel across his lap and bent forward, his eyes meeting Mary's. "I love you," he said, never meaning the words more than at that moment.

She sniffed and smiled. "I love you too," she whispered. Then, once again, the contraction hit.

"Okay, Mary, push," Bradley encouraged her. "Remember work with the contraction. Push down."

More of Mikey's head appeared, and Bradley waited for him to slide out. But the contraction ended, and he disappeared from sight. "That was so good," he said. "I could see so much more of his head this time. You're so close."

She nodded, breathing heavily, but didn't have the strength to answer him. "Here it comes," she gasped.

Bradley bent down and watched Mikey's head slowly appear, more and more of it showing. "Come on, Mary," he cried. "He's almost here."

Mary screamed as she bore down, and suddenly Mikey's head was out.

"His head is out," Bradley said, cradling the tiny head in his hands, tears running down his face. "His head is out."

Mary smiled. "Is he really a boy?"

Bradley laughed through his tears. "I can't tell yet," he said tenderly. "But one more push ought to do it."

She nodded and pushed as another contraction hit. Bradley felt the force of her muscles as the rest of the baby slid out into his arms. He wrapped the baby in the towel and used his finger to gently clean the mucus from the baby's mouth. Suddenly, a tiny wail echoed in the elevator box. Bradley lifted him up and put him in Mary's arms. "You did it," he said. "You were so amazing."

"He's so perfect," she cried, gently gliding her finger along his face. "He's a miracle."

Bradley nodded. "Yes, he is."

"Is everything okay down there?" Mickey called.

"Michael Timothy Alden was just born," Bradley said.

"Congratulations," Mickey said. "We're not going to worry about the umbilical cord just yet. You guys just cuddle that baby and relax for a little while."

"So, his birthday is January 12th," Mary said.

Bradley looked down at his watch and shook his head. "No, it's ten after twelve," he replied. "Mikey was born on Friday, January 13th."

Mary smiled. "A lucky day," she said.

"A very lucky day," he replied.

"I totally agree."

Mary and Bradley looked up in shock.

"Mike?" Mary cried. "Mike?"

He smiled at them. "I'm gone for a few days, and you decide to have your baby in an elevator?" he asked. "What were you thinking?"

Joy filled her heart while tears ran down her cheeks. "Everyone does a labor and delivery room," she said, her voice cracking with emotion. "How...How can you be back?"

"Well, I have a new assignment," he said. "But I couldn't show up until he was born."

"Mikey?" Bradley asked. "You're Mikey's guardian angel?"

Mike shrugged and nodded. "I had to beat up a couple of other angels to get the gig," he said. "But, you know, it was worth it."

He shook his head, and his eyes glistened with unshed tears. "Besides," he whispered, "you're family."

Chapter Seventy-six

"Are you still okay down there?" Mickey called down ten minutes later.

Bradley looked down at Mary, asleep in his arms and Mikey cuddled in her arms.

"We're great," he said, moderating his voice, so neither baby nor mom would be disturbed.

"Okay, then I'm stepping back so Mel can close this door and we can bring the elevator up to four," she said.

"Great," Bradley said. "Thanks."

A moment later the elevator lights came back on, and the box started moving. Mary opened her eyes. "We're moving?" she asked.

"Yes," he said, kissing her head. "We'll have you in a clean, comfy bed in a few minutes."

She smiled up at him. "I'm pretty comfy where I am right now," she replied.

He hugged her tighter. "You are exactly where you belong right now," he whispered.

The door opened, and they were met by several nurses and a gurney. Mary looked up at Bradley and smiled weakly. "Remember the last time I rode in one of those?" she whispered.

"Shhhh," he whispered back. "Our little secret."

Bradley slipped out from behind Mary and then knelt next to her. "Ready to go?" he asked.

She nodded, and Bradley scooped his wife and their baby into his arms and placed them both gently on the gurney. Mary looked back at the elevator and grimaced. "Sorry about the mess," she said.

The nurses laughed. "We've seen worse," one said. "Lots worse."

One of the nurses stepped into the elevator and picked up Mary's and Bradley's belongings. "I'll bring these along," she said. "You three just worry about each other."

They rolled Mary down the hallway towards the other set of elevators, right past Stanley's room.

"Wait," Mary called out.

They stopped immediately. "Is something wrong?" the nurse asked. "Are you feeling sick or dizzy?"

She shook her head. "I know this is unusual," she said. "But can we just make a quick stop?"

"A stop?" the nurse asked, confused.

Bradley chuckled and nodded. "Mikey's grandparents are in this room," he said. "We'd like to stop in and see them."

With a shrug, the nurse turned the gurney towards the door and knocked before she entered.

"Have you heard anything?" Rosie called out. "Is she…"

Rosie opened the door, immediately saw Mary holding the baby and started to cry. She hurried forward and hugged Mary tightly. "We were so worried about you," she said through tears. "Mel kept us informed, but to imagine you in an elevator giving birth…"

She looked down at the baby, cuddled against Mary's chest, and smiled. "He's just perfect, isn't he?"

Mary nodded. "Yes, he really is," she replied. "Is Stanley still awake?"

"Awake? He's been calling anyone he could think of to get you out of the elevator," she said, moving out of the way so the gurney could be pushed into the room. "Mel had to stop him from calling in the National Guard."

Stanley looked across the room, and his eyes filled with tears. "'Bout time they got you out of there," he grumbled, his voice thick with tears. He wiped a hand across his wrinkled face to dash away the tears.

"Are you okay?" he asked, his voice cracking.

Mary nodded as she wiped away her own tears. "I'm great," she said. "So great. I wanted you to meet Mikey."

They pushed the gurney as close as they could, and Stanley looked over from his bed to see the baby sleeping in Mary's arms. Then he shook his head and pushed his legs over the side of his bed. "I ain't gonna meet my newest grandson laying down like some invalid," he said.

"Stanley, no!" Rosie called, trying to get around Mary's gurney to him.

But Bradley was quicker. He stepped to Stanley's bedside. "You ain't gonna stop me," Stanley said, determination in his eyes.

Bradley shook his head. "No, sir, I wouldn't dream of it," he said. "But I would like to lend you a hand."

With glistening eyes, Stanley wrapped his arm around Bradley's shoulder, and Bradley gently helped him from his bed. They walked slowly, one step at a time, until Stanley was at Mary's side. He looked down at the baby and nodded, his lips trembling with emotion. "You done good, girlie," he finally said. "Real good."

Mary reached forward and hugged him. "Thank you," she whispered. "Thank you for being my extra dad."

"Okay," Bradley whispered to Stanley. "Ready to get back in bed?"

Stanley smiled at the younger man. "Reckon I'll get in all kinds of trouble if I don't," he said.

"Well, I know you're not afraid of trouble," Bradley said in a lowered voice. "But Mary is exhausted, and I know she won't want to leave if you're still up."

"Help me back then," he said quickly.

Bradley and Stanley walked slowly back to the bed. But Stanley stopped him before he helped him up. "Just wanted to tell you I'm proud of you, son," Stanley said. "You love that girl more than life itself, and I can see it. You did good tonight too. Proud to know you."

Bradley moved around and hugged Stanley. "Thank you," he said. "That meant the world to me."

They lowered the bed, and Bradley helped Stanley get back in and situate himself. Stanley looked over to Mary. "You go get some rest, hear?"

She grinned. "Yes, sir," she replied. "You too."

"Well I would if there weren't an entire circus in my room," he blustered with a smile. Then he lowered his voice. "Sleep well, girlie. You deserve it."

As they began to pull the gurney out of the room, Rosie came up beside Mary. "We've been texting with your mother all night," she said. "Both Mel and Mickey would give us updates, and we would share them with her immediately."

"Thank you so much," Mary replied, giving Rosie another hug.

Rosie held up her phone. "I think she would love a photo of all of you," she said.

Mary smiled and nodded. "Bradley, Rosie needs to take our picture for Ma," she said.

Bradley put his arm around Mary and smiled. "Now she might sleep tonight," Mary said.

He shook his head. "I kind of doubt it," he replied.

They pulled the gurney back out into the hall.

"Thank you," Mary said to the nurses. "That was so nice of you."

"After what you've been through tonight," the first nurse said, "that was the least we could do. Now let's get you to your room."

Chapter Seventy-seven

They stopped in front of the elevators, and Mary shook her head. "I have to admit I'm not looking forward to getting back into an elevator," she said.

Bradley put his hand on her shoulder. "But just remember the amazing things you accomplished last time you were in one," he teased.

She looked up at him. "I'm not quite ready for an encore performance," she replied.

"It will be a breeze this time," the nurse assured. "Besides, we really can't take the gurney down the steps."

"That's true," Mary said, taking a deep breath as the doors opened before them. "Okay, let's go."

The trip down to the second floor was done quickly and without incident. "Your doctor and Mickey will be waiting for you in your room," the nurse explained. "And your pediatrician is also there to give Mikey an exam."

"Perfect," Mary said.

The halls of the maternity wing were filled with lovely pictures of mothers and babies. The wallpaper was a soft pastel hue, and the lights were soft and dim. Mary slowly looked around. "This is so much prettier than the inside of an elevator," she said wistfully.

"Well, I think we'll be keeping you for at least a day or so," the nurse replied. "So, you'll be able to enjoy it."

The nurse punched in a security code, and the doors opened. Then she turned to Mary. "The doors are always locked," she said. "And family and friends are given a security code, or they can press this button and speak to the nurses station to gain entrance."

"That's nice," Bradley replied.He bent down and whispered to Mary, "Now I won't have to place armed guards on this floor to protect you and Mikey."

She smiled up at him. "I'm sure they will be relieved to hear that."

"Your room is right here, Room 222," the nurse said, pushing the gurney through the open door.

"Mary!" Margaret's voice rang through the room as she and Clarissa rushed forward to meet the gurney.

"Ma?" Mary exclaimed. "Clarissa? How did you get here?"

Bradley shrugged. "I may or may not have had one of my guys pick them up and drive them over," he said.

She smiled up at him, her eyes glistening. "Thank you."

Margaret hugged her daughter. "We were so worried about you," she said, brushing a tear from her cheek. "And look at you! More beautiful than I've ever seen."

Bradley leaned down and kissed Mary's head. "I agree," he said.

Clarissa came up on the other side of the gurney and gently touched Mikey's downy skin. "This is my brother?" she asked, her voice filled with awe.

Mary nodded. "Yes, this is Mikey," she said.

"Can I hold him?" Clarissa asked.

"Well, not yet," Mary replied. "Because the doctors still have to do a couple of things to him and to me. But soon, you'll be able to hold him."

"I'm sorry," the nurse said. "But we really need to have the doctors look at you."

"Well, Clarissa and I are going down to the cafeteria for a bit," Margaret said. She smiled at Mary. "Can I get you something to eat?"

"Oh, Ma, that would be wonderful," Mary said. "I could eat an entire buffet."

Margaret laughed. "Aye, I know that feeling well," she said. "Having a baby is hard work." She turned to Bradley.

"And for you?" she asked. "Because, I imagine helping with the birth is just as hard."

"I would love food," Bradley agreed. "Anything will be great."

"Okay, we'll be back in thirty minutes with food for both of you," she said.

Clarissa hesitated, holding onto the gurney. "Are you going to be okay?" she asked, worry creasing her brow.

Mary smiled and nodded. "I'm fine, sweetheart," she assured her. "There's absolutely nothing wrong with me."

"Are you sure?" she asked. "Mommy Jeannine died when I was born."

Bradley walked over and pulled Clarissa into his arms, holding her and rocking her for a moment. Then he released her and looked into her eyes. "What do you see on my face?" he asked.

She lifted her hand to his face. "I see a smile," she said. "All the way to your eyes."

He smiled wider and nodded. "Do I look worried?" he asked.

She shook her head. "No, you don't. You look so happy."

"I am so happy," he said. "Because Mary is safe, and Mikey is healthy, and nothing is going to happen to either of them."

She studied Bradley's face for a moment longer and then returned his smile. "I'm a big sister," she whispered happily.

He hugged her again. "Yes, you are," he said. "And you're going to be great at it!"

Chapter Seventy-eight

After giving Mary and Mikey clean bills of health, the doctors and nurses left Mary and Bradley alone with Mikey. They both watched in amazement as Mikey hungrily nursed for the first time.

"This is so unreal to me," Mary said.

"What do you mean?" Bradley whispered.

"Well, first, the whole idea that this baby I'm holding was inside of me just a few hours ago," she said. "I keep thinking, how the heck did he fit?"

Bradley chuckled. "As the official catcher, I can assure you that he did fit and that he did, indeed, come out of you," he said.

She laughed softly. "I know, but it seems so…I don't know, miraculous," she said. "And now, to be able to nourish him from my body. It's all so remarkable that it all works this way."

He nodded. "Yeah, this whole process has been remarkable," he said.

Mike appeared in the corner of the room, far enough away to give Mary and Mikey some privacy.

"It is more than remarkable," Mike said. "It really is a miracle."

"I'm so glad you're back," Mary said. "I feel like our family is whole again."

He smiled back at her. "I can't tell you how happy I am to be back," he replied. "But now, you have to decide something."

"What?" Bradley asked.

"Do you want Clarissa and Mikey to be able to see me?" he asked. "You two will still be able to see me. But, do you think having them being able to see me presents more problems than solutions?"

Mary shook her head. "I don't know," she admitted. "I would like to give Clarissa a chance to apologize to you. And I think it would be sad if Mikey never got to see you."

Mike smiled. "Well, Mikey is going be able to see me until he's about two years old," he said. "Babies can see angels for a while because they're so new to the earth. But then they grow up and become more a part of this world, so they lose that sight."

"So, normally, children wouldn't be able to see you," Bradley said. "After that age."

"Yes, although some of them still remember their angels," Mike said, "most don't." Then he grinned. "Obviously I would be one of the unforgettable ones."

"Obviously," Mary agreed. "What do you think?"

He sighed. "As much as I loved my interaction with Clarissa," he said, "I realized that maybe by always being there, she didn't have to rely on faith as much. She's prayed more, real prayers, since I left than she ever did before."

He shrugged. "She actually did pray for me," he said. "And tonight, Mary, she prayed for you and Mikey like she had never prayed before. And her prayers were answered."

"It will be weird, though," Bradley said, "not having that same interaction with you and the whole family. But, I see your point."

Mary turned to Bradley. "So, what should we do?"

"I think we need to take Mike's advice on this one," he said. "I think Clarissa needs to start understanding faith."

"Wow, there are going to be a lot of changes in our family," Mary said.

Mike met her eyes and nodded. "More than you even realize," he said.

"What?"

"They're coming back," he replied quickly. "Gotta go."

He disappeared just before Margaret and Clarissa came back into the room, their arms filled with take-out boxes from the cafeteria.

"Food," Mary sighed. "I've never been so happy to see food in my whole life!"

"Don't they feed you in the hospital?" Clarissa asked.

Mary laughed and nodded. "Yes, they do," she said. "But the next meal on the schedule is breakfast. And although they offered me some snacks, I could really use some real food right now."

Bradley rolled the hospital's food tray over next to the bed and unwrapped Mary's food. The smell of french fries and a grilled cheeseburger filled the room. "This is heavenly," Mary said, immediately biting into a french fry. "Thank you."

She scooted over on her bed. "Clarissa, do you want to climb up here and hold Mikey, while I eat?" she asked.

"Can I?" Clarissa asked, her eyes wide with wonder.

"Of course. You're the big sister," she said.

With Bradley's help, Clarissa climbed up on the bed and sat next to Mary. With her arm around her daughter, she gently placed the sleeping baby in Clarissa's arms. Clarissa bent over and kissed Mikey's head. "He so beautiful," she whispered.

Mary nodded, overwhelmed by the sight of her two children together. "Yes, it really is," she said.

A moment later, she reached over and took a bite of the hamburger. "This is so good," she sighed. "Thank you so much, Ma."

"You're more than welcome," Margaret replied. "And I just spoke with your Da. As soon as the roads are clear enough, they are coming up to see you and this new wee one."

"They?" Bradley asked.

Margaret grinned. "Aye, they," she said. "Da, Sean, Tom, Art and Ian. As well as Gillian and two ladies I haven't met yet— Brooke and Em."

"We're going to have a roomful," Mary said, and then she yawned.

Margaret walked over to the bed and looked down at Mikey, who was now sleeping soundly in Mary's arms. "He's an angel," she whispered. "I am so proud of you."

"Thank you, Ma," Mary replied. "I can't believe how much I love him already."

She kissed Mary's forehead. "Well, it only gets stronger," she said. "Now, you eat and then get some sleep. We'll be back mid-morning to see you.

And, I'll call your Da back and tell him that a noon visit would be best."

Mary smiled tiredly. "That would be great," she said.

Margaret hugged Bradley. "Thank you for taking care of my little girl," she said.

"She's my life," he replied simply.

Margaret smiled at him. "Aye, I know," she said. "And now, can you arrange another ride back home?"

"There's someone already downstairs waiting for you," he said. "He'll get you safely home."

"Thank you again," she said.

Clarissa reached up on the bed and hugged Mary. "I love you," she said.

"I love you too, sweetheart," Mary replied. "We'll see you in the morning."

After they left, there was a knock on the door and a nurse came in. "If you're done nursing Mikey," she said, "we can watch him in the nursery for a few hours while you sleep."

"Oh, that would be wonderful," Mary said.

"We'll wake you when he's hungry," the nurse replied. Then she turned to Bradley. "Do you need us to bring in a cot?"

Mary shook her head. "No," she interrupted, sliding over on the bed she was on. "I think there's room enough for two here."

Bradley smiled. "I'm not going to argue with that," he said.

The nurse turned the lights down low, and Bradley slipped off his shoes and climbed in next to Mary, holding her in his arms. "I love you, Mary," he said softly as sleep started to immediately overcome him.

She yawned back and then laughed. "I love you too."

Chapter Seventy-nine

"Darling, you look amazing," Ian said, brushing a kiss on her cheek. "And the wee bairn is like an angel. You never fail to impress me."

Mary smiled at Ian. "Well, now that you see how it's done, you and Gillian need to work on getting Mikey a cousin he can play with," she whispered to him.

He grinned at her. "Aye, and seeing her reaction to the babe," he said, "I might not have too much persuading to do."

"Hey, stop hogging all the time with my sister," Sean said, coming up alongside Ian. He smiled tenderly down at Mary. "You did good, kid."

She smiled up at her oldest brother. "Thanks," she said. "And your Em, she's lovely."

He nodded. "Yeah, she is," he said. "I'm amazed she agreed to come along. She's not really a people-person."

Mary studied him for a long moment. "She's not really an average person-person, is she?"

Shaking his head, he grinned at his sister. "No, she definitely is not," he agreed.

"I like her," Mary said. "So, I vote yes."

He leaned over and kissed her cheek. "That means a lot," he admitted. "Thank you. Now, I'm going to try and get a chance to hold the baby. Da hasn't let him go for ten minutes."

Ian looked around the room and then back at Mary, who was smiling at Tom's antics with Clarissa. "After things have settled down, can we talk?" he asked quietly.

She turned back to him. "Sure," she agreed.

As soon as he walked away, Art approached her bed. "You're kind of like a queen sitting on a throne as your royal subjects approach you," he teased.

She grinned and extended her hand. "You may kiss my ring," she replied in her best English royalty accent.

He bent down and hugged her. "You are amazing," he whispered.

She hugged him back. "I was scared to death," she whispered back.

"I bet you Bradley was even more scared," he said, remembering his feelings when he learned Brooke was alone with a killer.

"Well, if he was, he didn't show it," Mary replied.

"Didn't show what?" Bradley asked.

"Didn't show that you were more frightened than I was last night," Mary said.

"Well, yeah, I was much better once I was down in the elevator with you," he replied. "Discovering that you were missing was the most terrifying experience of my life."

Art nodded. "I totally understand," he said.

"I really like Brooke," Mary said. "She's really smart. How did she ever fall for you?"

Art chuckled. "Funny, funny," he replied. "I think it's my charm and wit."

"So, she's not as smart as she looks?" Mary asked with a grin.

"You are such a brat," Art replied.

Mary reached over and took her brother's hand. "Seriously, I think she's perfect for you," she said.

Art looked over his shoulder to make sure Brooke was distracted with something else and then leaned down and whispered, "Yeah, I think so too," he said. "Now all I have to do is convince her."

"Oh, when an O'Reilly sets his mind on something, there is no stopping him," Mary said.

"Amen to that," Bradley agreed.

"Well, what's a father have to do to get to see his little girl?" Timothy blustered.

Art winked at Mary and then stepped away from the bed. "Well, perhaps he needs to put his new grandson down for a moment," he replied.

"Ah, well, little Timmy is hard to put down," he confessed.

"Da, his name is Mikey," Mary reminded him.

"Ah, well, Michael Timothy," he said. "At least for now."

"What do you mean?" Mary asked.

"I'm bartering with your nurse to switch the names on the birth certificate," he announced. "I might have to mortgage the house, because she hasn't given in yet. But, I'm sure I'll convince her."

"When an O'Reilly sets his mind on something," Bradley reminded her.

She turned to Bradley, "Shhhhhh," she admonished. "Don't encourage him."

Timothy laughed and then bent over and enfolded Mary in a warm hug. "You are amazing, Mary-Mary," he whispered. "And little Mikey, he's a miracle, that's what he is. My heart is overflowing with joy."

"Thank you, Da," she whispered back, her voice thick with tears. "Thank you so much."

He kissed her head. "No, thank you, darling," he said. "You've made me the happiest father today. First, you gave me Clarissa and now Mikey. I'll tell you, there is nothing like holding your first grandson in your arms. It's a miracle, that's what it is, a miracle."

She nodded. "Thank you for coming," she said.

He stood up and looked amazed. "And you think we wouldn't come?" he asked. "I can tell you that we cleared the way for the snow plows, that's what we did. No snowstorm was going to stand in the way of me meeting my grandson for the first time.

Tom looked over his father's shoulder. "We really did, Mary," he agreed. "Da was driving like a maniac. We would have been pulled over, but no one could catch him."

Mary laughed. "Well, then, I'm glad you got here safely," she said.

Tom smiled down at his sister. "The risk was worth it," he said.

Timothy shook his head and stepped away from the bed. "Well, don't just stand there, you dolt," he grumbled. "Give your sister a hug while I go find my granddaughter and count my blessings."

Tom bent over and hugged Mary. "I love you, brat," he said.

"I love you too," she replied.

"May I have your attention?" Margaret's voice rose over the noise in the room, and everyone was suddenly quiet. "It's time for Mikey to be fed and for our Mary to take another nap. So, let's all retire to Mary and Bradley's house for lunch. Then, we can come back and visit this afternoon."

Like troops obeying their sergeant, the group said their quick goodbyes and left the room. Margaret came over to Mary's bed and laid Mikey in her arms. "Your father tried to take him with," she teased, and Mary laughed.

"You are glowing, but you still look worn out," Margaret continued. "So be sure to rest before we all descend upon you again."

Mary nodded, "I will, Ma," she said. "And thank you."

"I love you, darling," her mother said, placing a kiss on her daughter's cheek. "Now rest."

Chapter Eighty

A few minutes after they left, Ian came back in. "I sent Gillian ahead with Sean and Em," he said. "Because I need to talk to you."

"Sure," Mary said. "What's up?"

Ian gazed around the room. "Is Mike around?" he asked.

Mike appeared next to him. "Now he is," Mike said.

Ian met his eyes, and Mike nodded slowly. "You knew?" Ian asked.

"Yeah, I did," Mike said. "But I haven't said anything."

"What are you talking about?" Mary asked.

Ian turned back to her. "Okay, well, something odd happened in this room," Ian said. "And I wanted to talk to you about it."

"What happened?" Mary asked, confused.

"There were other…" he paused to find the right word. "People. Ghosts. Spirits… in your room."

"What?" Mary asked, surprised. "Where?"

"All around you," Ian said. "One woman told me she was your grandmother."

"Grandma was here?" Mary asked.

"And Jeannine was here, wishing you both well," Ian said.

"Jeannine was here?" Bradley asked.

"There were as many—" then he shook his head, "no, more people from the other side in this room, looking at Mikey, celebrating his birth, and wishing you well, than there were real people." He shook his head. "I mean, still living people."

"Wait. Why didn't I see them too?" she asked, and then she turned to Mike. "Why?"

"Because, Mary, you've been released from that responsibility," Mike explained.

"Released? I don't understand," she said, shaking her head.

"Mary, you have changed lives. You have unselfishly sacrificed your time and, often, your safety to help spirits move on," he explained. "And now, with Mikey here, your gift has been removed."

436

"Removed?" she gasped, tears forming in her eyes. "Did I do something wrong?"

"You aren't listening to me, Mary," Mike said. "You did everything right. But do you think, with both Mikey and Clarissa depending on you, that you could continue to do what you've been doing for these past few years?"

"I don't know," she said. "I could try."

"But God doesn't want you to try," Mike said. "He wants you to concentrate on your family. He wants you to be able to be a mom and a wife, without the extra responsibilities that have been yours lately."

"Just a mom?" she asked.

He glided towards her and stopped at the edge of her bed. "Just a mom?" he exclaimed. "Come on, Mary. You've been a mom for less than a year, but I know it's changed your life. Do you think there is any finer calling than being a mother? God had entrusted these little people into your care. You will be the person to guide them and help them learn right from wrong. You will be the first person they call out to when they're frightened. The first person they'll want to call when they have good news. The first person they'll need when their hearts are broken."

He smiled at her. "Being a mom is a full-time, twenty-four-seven job," he said. "Your other job was important, but not nearly as important as this one. You are not being punished. You're being promoted."

"But I loved what I did," she said. "I loved helping others."

"This is not a situation that will last forever," Mike said. "It's only for a season."

Mary studied him skeptically. "What does 'a season' mean?"

He smiled. "It's like a Mommy minute. The meaning matches the situation."

"A Mommy minute?" Bradley asked.

Mike's smile widened. "Remember when your mom was doing something, and you would call her name over and over again?" Mike asked. "And she would call back, I'll be there in a minute."

Bradley smiled and nodded. "Sometimes those minutes took a long time."

"Exactly," Mike said. "And Mary, you can be sure when God feels that it's the right time and the right place, your special sight will be opened up to you again. But, for now, you can just enjoy being a mom."

She looked down at the baby in her arms, who was starting to make a fuss because he was hungry, and then back at Mike. "I'm a little torn," she said. "Part of me feels this great sense of relief, like a burden has been taken off of my shoulders. But, another part of me feels like I'm going to be lost without doing what I do."

"Well, give it some time, Mary," Mike said. "I'll still be around. And when you feel ready to do this again, I'll petition on your behalf. Deal?"

"Deal," she said. Then she turned to Ian. "Thank you for telling me."

He smiled. "There was so much love in this room," he said softly. "I wanted to make sure you knew. You don't realize how many lives you've saved by your influence, including mine. I love the idea that you've been given a bit of a reprieve. Enjoy it while you can."

He leaned forward and kissed her forehead. "Now, feed that wee bairn and get some sleep," he said. "I'll see you this afternoon."

Ian left the room, and when he closed the door, Mike looked back at Mary. "Are we good?" he asked.

Mary nodded slowly. "Yes," she said. "I think we are."

"Love you," he said as he faded away.

"Love you too," she called after him.

She adjusted her hospital gown so Mikey could nurse and then looked over to Bradley. "What do you think?" she asked.

"Your gift brought us together," he said. "Your gift has saved my life. Your gift brought me my daughter and ended my search for Jeannine. I can never be anything but grateful for it."

He took a deep breath. "But, your gift has also put you in danger so many times," he said. "You risked your life for others, and you were always willing to do it. But, I have to admit I am grateful you don't have to do this for a while. I'm grateful that you can be a mother and whatever else you want to be. I'm grateful that you'll be safe. It's totally selfish, and I'll admit that. But you are our world, Mary, mine, Clarissa's and now Mikey's. You are everything to us."

"But you never said anything before," she said.

"How could I?" he asked. "I go out and risk my life every day. It's my job. It's what I do. How could I ask you to give it up?"

She sat back against the pillows, thinking silently for a moment, taking it all in. Could she still be Mary O'Reilly Alden and not do what she'd been doing? Could she be content with her life, without the magic of seeing the other side of the veil?

She looked down at Mikey and then over at Bradley, and her heart was filled with peace.

Yes, she thought. For now, she could be totally content.

The End

For Now

About the author: Terri Reid lives near Freeport, the home of the Mary O'Reilly Mystery Series, and loves a good ghost story. An independent author, Reid uploaded her first book "Loose Ends – A Mary O'Reilly Paranormal Mystery" in August 2010. By the end of 2013, "Loose Ends" had sold over 200,000 copies. She has sixteen other books in the Mary O'Reilly Series, the first books in the following series - "The Blackwood Files," "The Order of Brigid's Cross," and "The Legend of the Horsemen." She also has a stand-alone romance, "Bearly in Love." Reid has enjoyed Top Rated and Hot New Release status in the Women Sleuths and Paranormal Romance category through Amazon US. Her books have been translated into Spanish, Portuguese and German and are also now also available in print and audio versions. Reid has been quoted in several books about the self-publishing industry including "Let's Get Digital" by David Gaughran and "Interviews with Indie Authors: Top Tips from Successful Self-Published Authors" by Claire and Tim Ridgway. She was also honored to have some of her works included in A. J. Abbiati's book "The NORTAV Method for Writers – The Secrets to Constructing Prose Like the Pros."

She loves hearing from her readers at author@terrireid.com

Other Books by Terri Reid:

Mary O'Reilly Paranormal Mystery Series:

Mary O'Reilly Short Stories

The Order of Brigid's Cross (Sean's Story)

The Wild Hunt (Book 1)

The Faery Portal (Book 2)

The Blackwood Files (Art's Story)

File One: Family Secrets

File Two: Private Wars

PRCD Case Files: The Ghosts Of New Orleans -A Paranormal Research and Containment Division Case File

Eochaidh: Legend of the Horseman (Book One)

Sweet Romances

Bearly in Love

Sneakers – A Swift Romance

CPSIA information can be obtained
at www.ICGtesting.com
Printed in the USA
LVHW081058111118
596714LV00019B/730/P